LOOK BEFORE YOU JUMP

The Bartender Babe Chronicles
Book One

D. A. Bale

Look Before You Jump is a work of fiction. Characters, names, places, incidents, and organizations are a product of the author's imagination or are used fictitiously. Any resemblance to actual persons living or dead, business establishments, events, or locales is entirely coincidental.

Look Before You Jump
D. A. Bale
Copyright © 2022 D. A. Bale
Published by D. A. Bale

Cover design by GetCovers.com

All rights reserved. No part of this document or the related files may be reproduced or transmitted in any form, by any means (electronic, photocopying, or otherwise) without the prior written permission of the author.

ISBN: 1530584485
ISBN-13:   978-1530584482

ALSO BY D. A. BALE

<u>The Bartender Babe Chronicles</u>
Look Before You Jump
Think Before You Speak
Knock Before You Enter
Die Before You Wake
Aim Before You Shoot
Shoot Before You Blink

<u>The Deepest Darkness Series</u>
Running into the Darkness
Piercing the Darkness
Rising from the Darkness

The Study
a novelette

DEDICATION

To Toni

Because even though you eventually stabbed me in the back and stole twelve thousand dollars from me, it was the memory of our college trip to Dallas Alley and the Historic West End that became the germ that grew into this series.

For this and many other good memories from those days long gone, I thank you.

ACKNOWLEDGMENTS

There's no better feeling for an author than putting a book to bed – and there are no words great enough to praise the selfless souls who helped bring a novel to that state.

Thanks just doesn't measure up, but here's a big thank you anyway to the GK Brainstormers who are always the first to cut their teeth on the initial draft of all of my stories (even the ones that never made it to publication). Brian, Gary, Julie, Richard, and Tonya – Vicki would never have become as interesting as she is without your insight into the realm of humor. You've helped my stilted-at-birth funny bone to grow three sizes during the writing of this novel.

A great big thank you and digital air hugs go to my beta reading crew. Benette, Deb, and Sandra – you three will never know how much your ability to relate to and/or simply love Vicki and her antics helped resolve one of my critique group's biggest beefs with that character. As much fun as I had writing her and living vicariously through some of the memories she evoked from my college days, I worried about having gone too far.

Y'all helped me realize I hadn't.

CHAPTER ONE

They say life's challenges either make you bitter or better. In my case, there's a third option.

Bat-crap crazy.

But sometimes crazy can be good, the necessary catalyst for change. I know it was for my life all those weeks ago. Er, months? Okay fine, it's been a few years now.

Back then I had both feet firmly planted *over* the line. You know – ethics, morality, self-control, etcetera.

My ethics were at times questionable. More like in the interest of self-preservation.

My morals – can I plead the fifth?

Self-control? Yeah, you'll see where that got me in a minute.

The desire to practice a little control of self was what had me tilting at a certain windmill by the time that particular night rolled around and forever changed things in my self-absorbed existence. It's what brought my life *and* my Corvette to a screeching halt as I rounded the street corner to my apartment instead of spending it at someone else's.

Just wish I'd realized that little tidbit when I saw the blue and red lights near my apartment building flashing like a strobe on steroids. Same players – change direction.

But I digress.

Life prepared to teach me lessons. And for a hard-headed, smart-mouthed woman with a Texas-sized attitude only a mother could love, I had to learn them the hard way.

I knew I was in trouble even before opening my eyes.

The hangover headache shattered into my consciousness. Cotton mouth came next. Grit clouded my vision until sunlight batted it away like a sandblaster.

The early afternoon worsened when the unfamiliar surroundings came into focus. Floor to ceiling windows – I hated them very much at that moment – shimmered like heat waves off a parking lot in July. Industrial-style loft space opened beyond the railing of the upper floor bedroom.

So not my apartment. Too chic. Jealousy festered. Under different circumstances, I'd have enjoyed hanging out awhile in such surroundings.

Then the cold claws of panic gripped me as snippets of last night's rendezvous filtered into my sluggish brain. A groan escaped from someone – I can only assume me – as I sat up amid a cloud of white down comforter and tangled buff sheets, revealing my passed-out companion.

A chiseled face lay buried in a pillow, squared jaw under tousled brown hair looked like a luscious male model straight off the cover of a magazine. Not fair for a guy to look this good first thing in the morning.

Now if only I could remember the color of his eyes.

Strong broad shoulders graduated down to an amazing six-pack, slender hips, and – oh yum.

Awareness lurched before the headache returned to reclaim it. Oops, I'd done it again. Does forgetting the name of a sexual encounter make me a slut?

Don't answer that.

It was time to swear off men. Become a nun – well that was out of the question. I'd long ago relinquished virgin status. But if they could reconstitute orange juice, why couldn't I become a reconstituted virgin?

Either way, last night's obvious and unnamed entanglement would have to last me for awhile if I planned to practice celibacy anytime soon. At least I'd have the memories – that is, if I could only recall the guy's name.

As I slithered from the bed, the aches in my body told me we must have had a good time. The fact my strappy, four-inch heels were the only thing that had made it up to this floor suggested we'd had a *very* good time.

Bits and pieces of last night's wardrobe revealed themselves as I limped down the stairs and shrugged into them on my way toward the front door.

My keys looked like they'd been launched across the granite countertop of the bar, the stem on the cute little martini glass keychain broken beyond repair. My head thundered like a stampede as I tried to recall who had driven last night. I was barely coherent enough to drive this morning – or afternoon.

Oh hell. All I could think about was whether or not my Corvette had survived the trip in one piece. Perhaps I should take a vow of abstinence from not only sex but alcohol too.

Yeah, right.

A groan from upstairs. Time to make my stealth escape and vanish. I scurried – more like teetered and tripped – to the front door, carrying my heels and keys and praying to find my purse in the Vette.

A stealth escape? Let's just say if bartending didn't work out for me, the CIA or MI6 wouldn't be beating down my door anytime soon.

"What do you mean, you don't remember?"

My head threatened to crack like a champagne flute serenaded by a soprano, though I'd much rather just drink the champagne. Said soprano and best friend, Janine De'Laruse, could strip the peel off a potato with her squeal.

'Cept this time it felt as if it stripped the scalp from my skull.

I moaned. "Bring it down about twelve octaves, would you?"

"Most pianos only sport six octaves."

"Hanging up now."

"Spill, Victoria," Janine huffed. "I want details not excuses. A name. Number of climaxes. Types of positions. That sort of information. And don't you dare skimp out on me just because you've got a hangover the size of Texas."

"Ugh, you sound like my mother."

That silenced her for a split second. "When did you start talking to your *mother* about these exploits of yours?"

My mother. The thought got a chuckle out of me that sounded more like gravel in a blender. Talk to my mother about Mr. Yummy? Yeah, right.

If I even mentioned the word *sex* in conversation, my mother's head would explode. If it hadn't been for having little ol' me, I'd have suspected my mother of still being a virgin.

Hmm. Maybe I was adopted.

"No…calling me *Victoria* instead of *Vicki*," I grumbled, reaching into my fridge and pressing an ice cube against my temple. "It's irritating enough when my mom does it. I don't need it from my best friend too, especially after last night."

"You're really pissy when you've got a hangover." I could almost hear Janine's smirk.

"Some friend," I mumbled around a nibble of Oreo.

There's just something about a chocolatey cookie that settles the stomach – or it does for me. I guess that's why my pantry was full of them.

"So speaking of last night," Janine prodded, "give it up."

"I think I did enough of that last night."

The snicker echoed too loud through the connection. "You gave *it* up a long time ago."

"Don't remind me."

The thought jolted my sluggish and slutty mind back to that night more than ten years ago. The sex wasn't that great compared to what I now knew. But at fifteen, losing your virginity to the pastor's son wasn't such a bad way to go.

Breaking in the bed of his brand spanking new Ford F-150 dear dad had bought him for graduation, let's just say getting caught by the police with your pants down – or hanging from the tailgate, or tossed into the grass several feet from the truck – made the experience that much more memorable.

Eleven years later, I was still making experiences. Minus the memorable part.

"I tell ya," Janine said, interrupting my efforts to trip and traipse down memory lane. "The way you two were bumping and grinding on the bar top last night, I didn't think you'd finish dancing out the set before he took you right there."

"I have a vague recollection of dancing on the bar," I acknowledged.

Janine sighed. "What's the point of getting taken advantage of by gorgeous hunks of steamy man-flesh if you can't remember the experiences?"

"Let me get back with you on that when I have the brain capacity to figure out an acceptable answer."

A little bit of this and too much of that, I finally succeeded in putting an end to Janine's interrogation. I really couldn't blame her. The closest Janine has come to losing her virginity was when she hit an enormous pothole while riding our bikes when we were twelve.

If her mother had her way, Janine would still be a virgin even *after* her wedding night.

The ice cube had melted into a puddle that threatened to warp the fake wood kitchen floor. In my somewhat precarious condition, bending down to wipe it up almost sent me sprawling on my backside.

Laminate in the kitchen – whose bright idea was it to put wood by-products in a room dominated by water?

And when did I start sounding like a snooty impression of my parents?

For the millionth time that year – and it was barely June – I glanced around my little one-bedroom apartment with the laminate flooring, tattered and stained Berber carpet, and a cracked kitchenette countertop straight out of the eighties. I still loved every inch of it.

When you've grown up with anything and everything money, power, and status can buy, it was a bit difficult to go without the perks.

At first.

Now, after more than two years of freedom, it was hard to imagine giving up my independence to return to what I considered slavery. Eighties motif or not.

On occasion, Dad's voice still crept into my head – *why do you choose to live like a pauper?*

"Because I no longer have to bow and scrape to your sorry ass anymore, ol' Daddy dear," I said to the apartment walls only a tad too loud.

Slinky, my sweet tabby cat, didn't even flinch from his perch in the window well. The only species of the male persuasion who understood me, he stayed far away instead of tangling in my legs while I suffered through the effects of a hangover.

If only the other men in my life would take a lesson from Slink, my life would be a hell of a lot easier.

My dad's a ridiculously wealthy and powerful son-of-a-bitch.

Oops, sorry Grandma.

Like the Texas oilmen of yesteryear, Mr. Frank Bohanan cut his own trail in the industry with a lot of bribery, power plays, and just damn luck on his part. As a selfless philanthropist – emphasis on the self – he built the new building for the church we all had attended while I was growing up.

One of those mega churches. Seats ten thousand with video screens two stories high so you can get a really good look at what Pastor Dennis had for breakfast. Maybe Dad considered it some sort of penance to the congregation to make up for bringing me into their midst.

Nah. Probably more because it made for a great tax deduction several years running.

'Course *I* was considered the bad influence on the pastor's son when we got caught that night. Caused nothing short of a scandal to have the police catch us in the act in the bed of that F-150 and call our parents.

I still fondly remembered the ridges in that truck bed, jamming against my spine with each thrust.

Maybe I was the one who needed to do penance.

Did I or did I not take a vow of chastity after last night? Was I becoming my pubic – er, publicly benevolent father?

Perish the thought.

Dear Dad loved playing the saint on Sunday. That was after playing the Saturday night sinner. With Lisa. Or Lola. Or whatever the pick of the week was these days.

I tried to ignore the sperm donor and his revolving door of girlfriends these days.

Yup, like father like daughter. Only difference, he's married and acts as if he isn't. I'm not married and act as if I am.

In some ways.

One particular way.

But at least I can admit my sins of the flesh while he pretends to be the epitome of a Christian man.

Far from it. Believe me. I grew up in that household and had a front row seat to the train wreck of false smiles and hearty hugs, pretending to be the happy family when in reality life with my dad sucked ditchwater by the fathoms.

From prosperity theology to a God just waiting to play the Santa Claus Savior and fulfill all the demands of His saintly sinners, the sperm donor has ridden every theological bandwagon the televangelists proclaimed – and ridden at least half the women in the local congregation.

And trust me. In a church seating ten thousand a service, that's a lot of screwing around.

Okay, maybe I exaggerated a bit – it was probably closer to a smidge south of half.

Don't get me wrong. I believe in God. I just lack faith in the people He left in charge down here.

Then there's my Jezebel ways, and I'm not gonna juggle two different lifestyles simply to satisfy the morality patrol.

You know. The whole Saturday Sinner/Sunday Saint thing? Doesn't work for me.

Give me freedom. Or at least some semblance of it. I'm no William Wallace, that's for sure.

But I'm not above accepting an invitation to the occasional shopping jaunt to Macy's and Neiman Marcus with my mom and her no-limit credit card. Just because my dad and I have zero relationship doesn't mean I can't have one with my mother. How else could I afford my wardrobe on a bartender's salary?

Gee, does that make me sound shallow?

Don't answer that.

CHAPTER TWO

I usually looked forward to Tuesday lunches and shopping excursions with Mom every week.

Keyword *usually*.

It gave me a day to recover from my weekend extracurricular activities and before I had to head back to work on Wednesday nights.

I do love her for more than her credit card, mind you, even if we have a difficult time relating to one another outside the mall or boutique. Audra Elizabeth Bohanan, a respectable southern belle, gave birth to a holy hell-raiser – that described our relationship to a tee.

Secretly? I think Mom's proud of me for standing up to my dad.

It was more than she's been able to do. Mom deserves everything sainthood promises for putting up with her husband. Why she hasn't left him I'll never understand, though it'd be awfully hard to live without the luxurious standards she's grown accustomed to after all these years.

This I know firsthand.

Then there's the whole scandal of divorce, which in her circle would create even more problems. After being the public face of disgrace for my family, I know what I'm talking about here.

Difference was, I just didn't care anymore.

Mom, on the other hand, also once sported the title of Miss Texas and would never do anything to taint that proud heritage. With long elegant legs and exotic green eyes that put the 'eyes' in *Irish eyes are smiling*, it's easy to see how she won the pageant that year. Even with the great genes I inherited from her side, you'd never catch me dead in some beauty contest.

Okay, maybe dead. But I'd be resisting in spirit form and haunting the hell out of whoever put my body up to it, I'm telling you.

But I digress.

Lunch and shopping were made for mothers and daughters. Quite literally it seems. Having Janine show up only doubled the fun.

If only my best friend didn't have *her* mother in tow, I'd have yelled out a hearty *howdy* like a good Texan. But the presence of Mrs. Thomas De'Laruse – Charlotte to my mother – did not bode well for fun and frivolity.

Hence the *usually* in how I felt about all but this particular Tuesday excursion.

Besides the biggest hair in all of Texas – and that's saying something around these parts – Mrs. De'Laruse sported the deepest Louisiana drawl this side of the Mississippi. The wealthy De'Laruse clan was one of few who'd successfully transitioned after the Civil War. Now they weren't only rich, they were *filthy* rich.

'Course some say her great-great grandfather colluded with the Union, resulting in the reprieve that was granted to their plantation mansion instead of it becoming a pile of charred and blackened ashes like so many of the others.

Charlotte then added to the family tradition of breeding whispers behind closed doors by eloping with a man of solid Creole stock – but Janine and I are prohibited from mentioning the eloping part in conversation.

So instead of dear old Papa De'Laruse throwing him into the bayou as gator bait, Thomas received a thorough education and grooming in what it would require to someday take over the family financial empire.

'Course that was only after agreeing to drop his surname in favor of the De'Laruse name. I guess some traditions are okay to toss out the window in today's hyphenated world.

"Victoria, dawlin'," Mrs. De'Laruse drawled as she returned her teacup to the saucer like a well-trained debutante. "What's been keepin' you so busy on Sunday mornings you can't make it to church anymore? I haven't seen you there in, what, a year?"

More like two, but I wasn't even gonna attempt a correction.

"Yes, *Victoria*." Janine leaned forward and batted her baby-doll blue eyes. "Do tell."

Before I could voice the smart-aleck retort bubbling up inside me, a swift kick to my shin lodged a piece of chicken avocado sandwich in my throat. All I got out was a quick cough before Mom stole my moment right out from under the table.

Quite literally too.

"She's still trying to get that boss of hers to let her off earlier on Saturday nights."

My mom was either a more practiced liar than I'd given her credit for, or she'd convinced herself of its truth to assuage that pesky mother's guilt.

The pain in my shin, however, had me leaning more toward the former instead of the latter.

Mrs. De'Laruse nearly snorted tea into her lungs. "I don't see why you feel the need for a job in the first place, Victoria. A woman of good breedin' needs only a good man."

Janine's eyebrows came close to disappearing into her blonde hairline. "Hear that, Vicki? A good man."

If I could've untangled my new tangerine pumps fast enough, I'd have sent a little of Mom's message Janine's way.

'Cept in her case, I'd have gone in with both barrels.

Her mom beat me to the punch. "What would you know about a good man, Janine? You're wastin' away chasin' this doctorate dream of yours. Look at you. Almost thirty and turned down every prospect you've ever had."

"I'm only twenty-six, Mama."

"And unmarried still," Mrs. De'Laruse continued with nary a breath. "What's the world come to, my dawlin' Audra, when young ladies refuse to marry until they're beyond child-bearin' years?"

"Mama!" Janine's face reddened – and probably not from the heat and humidity this fine Texas summer.

Mom interceded. "With good health and diet these days, women are still within child-bearing capacity well into their forties, Charlotte."

Chalk one up for intelligent, well-informed mothers everywhere.

Part of me begged for my mother to use the word *fertile*. It kinda has a bit of a sexual tone to it, don't you think? But that's something my mother doesn't acknowledge.

Hell, neither mother used the term *pregnant* and instead referred to women as *with child,* as if all pregnant women were as virginal as the Virgin Mary.

"Speakin' of children," Mrs. De'Laruse continued like a dog chewing the last morsel from its bone. "Were you aware that Pastor Dennis's son, Robert, has returned from parts unknown?"

Robert? Did she mean *my* Robert – er, Bobby? The man I gave my virginity to who summarily turned tail and ran away from home, leaving me to face the firing squad alone? *That* Robert?

"And," Mrs. D resumed, "he brings along a wife *with child.*"

What'd I tell you?

"Why no, Mrs. De'Laruse," I responded, raising a brow in Janine's direction. "No one told me."

"Robert is *married,*" Mom emphasized between bites of spinach leaf and strawberry salad. "With a *child* on the way."

As if I was deaf.

Janine picked up where her mother left off. "Pastor Dennis wants to start the process of grooming him to take over the senior pastorate at the church when he retires someday."

That stopped the teacup on the way to my mouth. Good thing I hadn't yet taken a sip, because I'd have ended up spraying it all across the table.

Mom tried teaching me good manners – honest she did. In my case, it wasn't so much the teacher as the student.

"Bobby's a *preacher*?"

"Really, dear," Mom clucked. "Do you listen to nothing I say? He graduated from seminary several years ago."

"I thought you said he went to the cemetery."

There were times after Bobby left that I wanted to personally put him there. In a grave. Dug to China. But I'd finally gotten over the heartbreak and forgiven him.

Cross my heart.

After all, I understood the pressures he'd faced under the constant eye of the Sanctimonious Saved and couldn't blame him for looking for the escape hatch.

However, now the thought of seeing him again sent an involuntary flutter from my heart all the way to my nether regions.

But Bobby – a pastor?

Nope, still didn't compute.

Janine interjected before my mother could berate me further. "He's gonna start as the pastor of the children's department."

"But he'll quickly move up to somethin' more worthy of his family name," Mrs. De'Laruse finished.

Janine smiled over the lip of her teacup – a devious, cunning, and very wicked smile directed my way. "Will that get you up for church next Sunday, or what?"

Or what indeed.

I have an innate ability to walk into Neiman Marcus and zero in on the party-girl section. You know, where they keep the leathers, laces, and things that make you want to go bump in the night.

In this case I mean dancing. The stuff that comes later doesn't involve clothes.

The shopping assistant met us inside the store and after introductions, whisked us off toward shoes, which took Mom and I right past my favorite department. A momentary slowdown offered a view of a great leather sheath dress that would be perfect at my job. Pair it with some thigh-high boots, and I'd look like a dominatrix right out of a movie.

'Course Mom would never agree to such attire.

Willingly, that is.

During the last few years of working at the bar, I'd had to get creative with my wardrobe. What was a tasteful, long top or blouse to Mom became a mini-dress to me.

A peek-a-boo lacy overlay? Forget the underlying camisole and let the lace speak for itself, I always say. What good are colorful and decorative bras if you don't get to show them off once in awhile?

"You coming, Victoria?" Mom called, having stopped up ahead.

"Yeah," I responded, somewhat despondent. "These new heels aren't as comfortable as I thought."

Don't judge me for the little white lie.

Mom looked down at the new tangerine pumps she'd purchased just that morning to go with the *appropriate* summer dress she'd bought me the week before. When it comes to shopping, luncheons, or just leaving the house, Mom always says a woman should look her best because you never knew who you'd chance to see.

Hell, every Tuesday's outing I looked dressed up enough for Sunday church. Too bad my attitude didn't match the attire.

Mom tsked. "We'll have to find a more appropriate pair while we're here then."

The solution to everything in Mom's book? Dispatch the old and buy something new.

Sometimes I missed the days of not having to worry about balancing a checkbook or saving for new tires on the

Vette. But freedom came with a price – one I was glad to pay if it meant not having to deal with the sperm donor.

The clothes Mom bought me every week? Let's chalk that up to the price a mother wished to pay to spend time with her daughter. I really tried not to take advantage of her generosity.

Most of the time.

While checking out at one of the registers toward the end of our shopping excursion, Mom noticed a lovely little floral number she just had to try on, which left me standing there with a pile of clothes and shoes that rivaled the heights of the Matterhorn.

And I ain't talking at Disney, folks.

I nearly piddled in my panties when she handed me the black, no-limit AmEx and waltzed away with the personal shopping assistant toward a dressing room.

My eyes locked with the clerk's. "I'll be right back."

With a potential three to five minute window, I sprinted across the store in my brand-brand new tangerine pumps. I grabbed the size four black leather sheath and saw the matching studded bolero jacket I just had to have.

Hey, it was part of an ensemble.

Then my roving eye caught the platinum-colored, barely there lace dress they happened to have in my size as well. New bar-appropriate attire in hand, I raced like a pursued purse snatcher back to the previously vacated register.

I was surprised someone hadn't sicced security on my fast fanny.

The register clerk cast me a knowing grin when I handed over the confiscated items and asked her to ring them up ASAP. The good sales chick even hid them between several other items among my hang-up bag.

Somebody needed to give that girl a raise.

Mom returned as the clerk finished subtotaling the existing pile then added in the flowing pink dress, something for church or the ladies Thursday luncheon. Like a dutiful daughter, I then handed over the credit card to my mother.

"You seem winded, Victoria," my mother observed. "Do you need to use my inhaler?"

I smiled. "I'm good, Mom. Just excited over some new clothes."

Am I a little dickens or what?

Don't answer that.

CHAPTER THREE

Wednesday nights at the bar tended to rev up kinda slow, the band's music levels allowing orders placed in an almost normal tone of voice.

My boss slow to rev? Not so much.

I recognized the press of Grady's warm lips across my bare shoulders. Even though I knew it was coming at some point, it still made me jump every time he snuck up on me like that.

"Nice to see you too, Grady," I responded.

Deep brown eyes penetrated mine like liquid chocolate you just wanted to dive right into. A lopsided smile tipped one edge of his mustache higher than the other. The man oozed charm.

And pheromones.

He was handsome and knew it, but I had a rule about tangoing between the sheets with the man who signed my paycheck.

Okay, yeah it's all direct deposit nowadays, but I still wasn't getting involved with the boss man.

No matter how much my noodle-like legs protested.

Grady trailed his finger lightly down my arm as he leaned against the bar. "You can see more of me anytime ya want, Vic. All's ya gotta do is say the word."

I shoved his hand away and busied finishing a customer's cocktail. "Some might construe this as sexual harassment."

"What would ya call it?" Grady's husky voice whispered in my ear.

I shivered and nearly dropped the drink before I handed it over to the patron and collected payment.

Every night it was the same, this dance of ours where Grady advanced and I retreated like a waltz in two-two time instead of three-four time, as Janine would say. After the last two and a-half years, I'd come to enjoy our little repartee. All in good fun without letting things get complicated.

Plus, on the rare occasion when Grady didn't start the evening out this way, I knew he was pissed about something – or *at* someone.

Sometimes I did things on purpose just to get a rise out of him if he was being too laid back. Showed him I still held *some* power, even though he could fire my lily-white ass anytime he wished.

I ignored his question and steered him toward one of my own. "What'll you have tonight, boss?"

"The usual."

Without glancing away from his warm stare, a flick of the wrist to insert the shot glass into my cleavage before I grabbed the Jack to pour. I'd perfected this little technique so well I didn't even have to see the glass to know when the whiskey reached three fingers.

And I didn't dare spill a drop. Too much temptation for Grady to mop up the drips from my chest with his tongue.

Or perhaps that was too much temptation for me.

The other side of Grady's mustache joined the first as he retrieved the glass from its resting place between my boobs. The feather brush of his fingers against my skin sent chills up my spine.

He stared down the length of me before knocking back the drink in one swallow. "New dress?"

"Yeah," I said a mite breathy. "A gift from my mom."

Not quite a gift per se. Mom never would've willingly purchased the strapless sheath that hugged me tighter than a lover and pushed up my Texas-sized bosom until it was almost spilling over the top of the black leather. We'd have to chalk this one up to yesterday's ingenious planning.

Or just downright sneakiness.

Grady offered another appreciative glance at my leather-clad cleavage. "Your mom's got good taste."

If he only knew about my in-store sprint. "Speaking of moms, I'm gonna need off this Saturday night."

That earned me a groan.

"Come on," I prodded. "In two and a-half years, when have I asked for a day off?"

"Countin' last month?"

"Besides that."

Grady pushed back his Stetson and rubbed a hand across his forehead. "You're killin' me, Vic."

"Everyone's here on Saturdays. You've got Bud and Wanker for behind the bar, and Rochelle and Baby can handle the guys on the floor without me for once."

"The guys come just to see what you'll do next."

The list of my Saturday night antics was long and distinguished – or not.

Dancing on the bar in barely there skirts resulted in actual monetary bets placed of Guess the Color of that

Thong. Kissing contests, drinking contests, and impromptu wet t-shirt contests from *accidental* beer spills completed my repertoire.

Maybe it was time to come up with some new material.

I turned the bottle of Jack upside down and let two fingers of smooth whisky slide down my throat. Grady held out his shot glass and joined me in downing another round.

"Was the dress a bribe to get ya to church on Sunday?" Grady asked.

"You might say that."

An exaggerated sigh. "Go make your mom happy then."

I gave Grady a kiss on the cheek. Then he handed me the empty shot glass and left the bar area to mingle with some of the regulars before heading to his office to do paperwork. It gave me a chance to watch his tall, slender form from the backside.

The back. I meant from the back.

Before I finished enjoying the view, a trio of guys sauntered over and sat along the bar looking as ruffled as the Cowboys offensive line after a quarterback sack. All three appeared frayed at the edges after long days slaving away in the corporate world, young egos bruised by reality.

Time for a little fun.

"What'll it be?" I began in my tired bartender banter. Before any of them mumbled an order, I put up a hand. "Wait. I'll bet I can guess."

That brightened their attention and earned me a smile from one, a smirk of derision from another, and a penetrating stare from the third.

"Prove it," the third challenged.

Thing Three loosened his run-of-the-mill cobalt tie and unbuttoned the two top of his white Perry Ellis dress shirt.

The black straight-off-the-rack suit jacket screamed department store, while black hair sported a classy cut and style of one trying to impress his elders.

The steady gaze from blood-shot eyes and the firm line of the lips bespoke a customer who knew how to play it cool and close to the chest while in the midst of an all-nighter of poker – or chicken. A confident character. Someone unafraid of facing life's challenges head-on.

I laid down a napkin in front of him and leaned forward. His dark eyes didn't leave mine even with my pushed-up assets in view.

"Lawyer," I began. "Associate with a big name firm and equally big aspirations. Putting in the hours and plan to make partner by the time you're thirty."

The stare never wavered, though a brow hiked up ever so slight. "Nice."

I'm pretty sure he meant my guess and not the assets. I offered a grin before pulling away. "Though you might consider having that suit tailored before your next court appearance. Been missing a few too many meals, by all accounts."

His veneer cracked. "I'll do that." Thing Three grabbed a handful of peanuts and popped one in his mouth with the slow tilt of a smirk. "Now what about that drink?"

Smooth and cool drink for a smooth and cool customer. "Scotch on the rocks."

That earned me a full-blown smile and a slap on the bar. "Make it so, counselor."

"How'd you do that?" Thing Two asked with an incredulous grin.

"A good magician never shares her secrets," I said as I poured then handed over the drink.

"Okay, you've gotta do me next," Thing Two said in a silky voice.

Do him next? No problem.

Relaxed. Easy-going. Thing Two nonchalantly rubbed his earlobe like a rabbit's foot or some other good luck charm. Deep impressions flattened his amber hair as if a pair of glasses had sat there all day – or a headset.

A kaleidoscope of color meandered across the rumpled button-down with the sleeves cuffed to his elbows. I'd noticed it hanging untucked from his jeans before the trio had bellied up to the bar. A fun guy who didn't put on airs, with a voice made for television and a wardrobe made for radio.

I liked Thing Two already.

I wiped down the spot in front of him and stared into cornflower-blue eyes before finalizing my decision. Too comfortable in his own skin and not neurotic enough for television. And with that voice?

"You're in radio."

Eyes widened before he threw his head back with a husky laugh. "That's uncanny."

"So I'm right?"

"Creepily so. I do the *Live on the Drive at Five* segment and all the other shit they throw at me down at the station."

"How'd you get on the air so early in your career?" I popped the top of a Sam Adam's Summer Ale and set it before him.

Thing Two – no, Radioman – took a deep pull, giving me a view of his Adam's apple as it bobbed up and down.

The movement sent tingles to my nether regions. And I'd thought his voice was enough to curl my toes.

Yeah, I'd definitely be willing to do him next. Hmm…

He finished the swig and stared at me over the rim. "Must be my voice."

"Mmm...I'll bet."

The timbre had me purring already as I leaned an elbow on the bar and rested my chin in my hand. Radioman followed suit – and didn't hesitate to let his gaze wander downward before drawing up to mine again with a sexy grin.

Was it getting warm in here?

Scratch that – more like volcanic.

"I'm still waiting," Thing One called out.

After breaking the trance Radioman had placed me under, I wasn't in the mood to size up the final patron. But one glance told me this guy would be the easiest to peg.

Practiced smile didn't reach calculating eyes. Chilled but not yet glacial. Sell out his mother but not his best friends.

Yet.

Fair hair already thinning and plastered against an oily forehead coupled with a clenched jaw bespoke the stresses of middle management. The impeccably tailored midnight-blue suit along with the still well-anchored tie gave new meaning to the words *stiff* and *uptight*.

Probably a bit OCD – or a lot – but a definite hard drinker when the day's work was done. How else could this guy relax and forget the misdeeds of the day?

"Jack and Coke," I said. "Straight up for the banker."

"Make it a double," Thing One commanded without blinking. "And I'm in investments, not banking."

"Oh really?" I challenged. "And where's your office?"

Under the stare of friends, Thing One finally squirmed. "First National downtown."

Raucous laughter filled their end of the bar.

I raised my hands in triumph after setting his drink on the counter. "I rest my case."

I didn't even get the teeniest drop of acknowledgement or praise – and little more than a paltry tip when Thing One laid down his cash. Yep, cheapo banker dude. Won't hesitate to spend money to make himself look good but maintains a death grip on the wallet around others.

I'd hate to be his server at a five-star restaurant. He'd calculate the tip down to the penny – if he left one at all.

The music level rose as I bopped and spun my way down the bar to help other customers drown their sorrows and soothe away the day's anxieties.

I loved my job.

Outside Janine, for the first time in my life I felt like I had real friends here, not those plastic banana smiles and wimpy hugs followed by blazing gossip I'd encountered growing up in the church. Life was hard enough without the stage performance every Sunday.

Being noticed all the time merely because of personal affiliation and under constant scrutiny by Club Holier-Than-Thou made me suspicious of motive when anyone tried to weasel their way into my world. I hated how cynical I'd become, which was why I'd decided to make some serious changes in my life.

I wasn't interested in riding the hypocrite train like my dad or being fodder for gossip ala Mrs. De'Laruse. After all those years, I'd nearly bled out from repeated back-stabbings from supposed *friends*.

At the bar I'd found real friendships. Well, and the occasional one-night-stand. But I was finished with those. For now.

At least for a little while.

Here I was finally home. At peace among the pulsating beat, the neon lights and the white silk streams hanging down from the ceiling against the backdrop of walled nighttime. Grady had strategically placed the silk along the ceiling close to the air vents so it writhed like ethereal specters in the darkness.

I'd love to do something like it in my apartment bedroom, but the look would be completely out of place in my outdated hole. Plus, if I started on the bedroom the whole place would need a major overhaul, something I could scarce afford.

Then there was the landlord, who might not take too kindly to such an eclectic look if I ever moved out. Say goodbye to that deposit.

Now Mr. Yummy from Saturday night? I could definitely see such a look fitting in with the industrial yet sexy motif of his condo.

"Hello again there, love."

"What'll it be?" I started in with my bartender banter.

Could've wiped the floor with my jaw when I glanced up to see the hunky Saturday night sleepover sidled up to the bar.

The mussed hair looked just like it did when I'd awakened Sunday afternoon to the walk of shame. But this time the brown locks hung over his forehead instead of brushed away from it. Definite GQ material screaming off the pages.

'Cept this one was live and in the flesh – with a sexy Aussie accent to boot. How could I have forgotten those ice-blue eyes? A girl could get lost in them.

Waking up Thursday morning in his apartment, I realized once again that I had.

At least this time I remembered Nick's name.

CHAPTER FOUR

"Every night this week?"

Janine's eyes threatened to pop out of her head. Instead of drool she dribbled popcorn onto my outdated couch and stopped petting my kitty on her lap to pause the movie. Even in our mid-twenties it was still fun hanging out in our PJ's eating popcorn and Oreos and talking about boys like two pre-pubescent girls.

'Cept now it was about men.

"Not *every* night," I corrected.

She pursed her lips like a true De'Laruse.

"Just since Wednesday," I grudgingly admitted. "But tonight I'm spending with you."

The gigantic popcorn bowl came between us. "Don't get any ideas there, princess. I may still be a virgin, but I have eyes only for men."

"Very funny," I said, reaching into the bowl and hammering Janine with a popcorn bombardment.

Slinky launched off her lap with a yowl and skittered across the floor away from the battle. Served my traitorous tabby right. The popcorn fight kept us occupied for about thirty seconds until the bowl emptied.

Hey, not like it's cookie dough or anything. Get the vacuum cleaner out and two minutes later, voila. Popcorn gone without a trace. It's the best food fight money can buy.

Janine ran her finger along the empty bowl's edge and licked off the last vestiges of the butter from her fingers. "Seriously though, are you boyfriend and girlfriend now, or are you just hooking up with Nick? When do I get to meet him?"

"Whoa there, Nellie. None of that there 'b' word. That's a flippin' curse word among these here walls."

Truth be told, I was rather ashamed of myself for my lack of willpower when it came to Nick. There was something about the way his ice blue eyes penetrated mine. The way his luscious and pouty lips would curl just before he captured my lips, not to mention the heat that sucked away the air from around us 'til I couldn't breathe.

Every time he neared, I felt like I was in a trance. Our bodies were drawn together like magnets and nothing would force us apart.

Until I awoke the morning after.

I had yet to stick around for him to wake up, much less share breakfast after our nightly romps. That bespoke an intimacy I no longer wanted to entertain.

Ever again.

"Besides," I continued. "I've always been a sucker for yummy accents."

"Not the only thing. Seems you're a sucker for yummy…"

"That too," I interrupted. "But there's more to life than just sex."

Did that statement just pop out of *my* mouth?

"Ugh, I have no life." Janine groaned.

I'm not sure what I did would at times be considered a life either, though it somehow held a glow of merit to Janine. Call me Mary Magdalene to her Virgin Mary.

"Hello," I responded, tossing an Oreo her way. "Who's the little miss getting a doctorate while one of us plays bartender?"

"Exactly! Teaching Dr. Husingkamp's students by day and studying by night makes for a mundane existence." Kernels of unpopped corn peppered the carpet as she tossed the bowl aside. "I'd give anything to let it all go for one week and live a life of freedom like yours."

"What do you mean? You visit at the bar some Saturday nights."

"Yeah, and have to race home by midnight before I turn into a pumpkin," Janine whined. "I can't even drink anything but pop or risk my mom's wrath. That woman can smell alcohol tinged breath in the next county."

"Living with the parents must suck."

"I'm so tired of being treated like a twelve-year-old. I want to have some fun without worrying about repercussions. Smoke a cigarette. Drink myself under the table – or into someone's arms. Experience a night of unbridled passion." Janine sighed. "Do you think doctors can put a hymen back together once it's broken?"

"Not like it's Humpty Dumpty or anything."

Janine slumped against the armrest pillows like a drama queen. "I'm doomed to forever remain a virgin, Vicki. My only hope in this world is living vicariously through your adventures and amorous activities with your boyfriend."

"Again with the b-word thing," I cautioned. "The last one cured me of that title."

"Keeping options open, are we?" Janine's brows went north so fast they almost crossed the Mason-Dixon Line. "Anyone I know?"

The innocent act never worked with me. I knew what the less-than-subtle girl was getting at – something to do with an F-150 driven by the pastor's son.

"Bobby's married, remember?" I reminded. "And a pastor."

"It won't hurt to look. Y'all have a history, if I do recall, only now Bobby's got an SUV instead of the F-150."

"He's got a pregnant *wife* now too. As in till-death-do-us-part."

"Pish-posh," Janine returned like a true De'Laruse.

"I don't do married men, Janine."

"Well, there was that time…"

"He conveniently forgot to mention that and failed to wear a ring," I huffed. "*And* we agreed never to speak of it again."

"Fine," Janine grumbled.

Attention returned to the sappy movie Janine had brought with her. After suffering through my collection of mystery, horror, sexy slasher, and shoot 'em up cop thrillers over the years, my best friend made me suffer through hers in return. She had a more delicate and sensitive palate in need of girlie romance where love triumphed over all.

They just made me gag. Romance was bo-o-ring, and so unrealistic. Where was the action? Adventure? The blood?

Janine piped up again. "What're you gonna do when you see him at church in the morning?"

"Smile and say 'howdy' like a proper Texan."

The movie held her attention for all of thirty seconds before Janine whispered, "I got to see him this week when he was setting up his office."

"That's nice."

"He's still got all his hair."

For a split second the movie shifted and all I could picture was my fingers entwined in blond hair in the bed of that F-150. A phantom ache started in my lower back.

Then it dropped even lower.

Janine interrupted my scandalous memory. "He's even more handsome than he was in high school."

"Hey," I said, scratching my hip. "I'm watching a movie here."

"No you're not. You hate romance."

"Then stop bugging me so I can sleep through it."

Moments later. "Nervous about seeing him again?"

Nervous? Try terrified.

Showing up at church tomorrow after an absence of two years would provoke a chorus of wagging tongues loud enough to interrupt Heaven's chorus of angels.

However, I was not going there to put on a show for anyone else's benefit. I was not attending church tomorrow for the first time in years to play the saintly hypocrite.

After avoiding one another following the firestorm eleven years ago, coupled with the lack of Bobby's return after college, I simply felt it was time to set things right between us. He needed to know I'd forgiven him and moved on.

What better place to offer that than in church, surrounded by a cloud of ten thousand witnesses?

"Nervous?" I repeated. "Nah."

Lord, don't strike me down for lying.

CHAPTER FIVE

It's amazing how territorial the human race can be.

Even after my lack of church attendance since moving out, my parents still sat in the same seats – third row from the front, left of center section. I'm not sure if Mom saved the extra theatre-like chair every Sunday in hopes of seeing me attend again, or if she did so this time because she knew I was coming.

In order to avoid the unpleasant fakery of my dad and the surprised glances of the Holy Huddlers, I made a point of dragging in late with a worried Janine. The rock concert atmosphere of flashing lights and strobe effects while the band performed for the masses kept most eyes from focusing in on us.

Janine hauled me down center aisle, making a beeline for our families like a wide receiver clutching the pigskin and barreling toward the end zone. The glacial stare she received from her mother as she took her seat among the De'Laruse clan explained the rush more than words ever could – not that you could hear anything over the music.

I received a genuinely surprised smile from my mother while avoiding a glance from Mr. Sperm Donor.

Another thing I was thankful for? I didn't have to endure the pressure of conformity to a household standard. Well, a standard that applied to everyone 'cept my dad.

Or me, since moving out on my own. But I felt sorry for Janine.

Our tardiness was my fault, centered on a selfish agenda of avoidance. I hadn't stopped to consider how our late arrival would create a problem for my best friend. Her constant references of the time should've been my clue.

Am I dense sometimes or what?

Don't answer that.

For the next hour or so, I stood and sat in the right places, clapped and tried to remember the words to the songs – most of which were new to me – and tried to avoid vertigo while staring up at Pastor Dennis's image on the massive movie screens surrounding the auditorium. It took concentration to keep my eyes fixed on the real-life image on the stage directly ahead instead of succumbing to shiny-object-syndrome and mindlessly staring at the screens like watching TV.

With all the effort, I couldn't begin to tell you the content of his sermon. If the past was any indicator, it probably went something like *blah, blah, blah, give, blah, blah, blah, money, blah, ask, blah, get* – and don't forget to leave your wallet on the way out.

That last part was my paraphrase, but you get the drift. Same dance. Come back next week. And be sure to bring a new wallet full of Benjamins.

When the lights came up after the final number, the congregants jostled en masse to make way for the third service. The whole thing really was like a movie theatre or rock concert experience. I'd forgotten some of that in my absence.

Janine grabbed my arm once again and shoved me through the throng to the gathering point, a three-story glassed-in tower everyone congregated in before and after each service. It acted kinda like a cattle holding pen with a trough of refreshments. When you're talking about a room that seats ten thousand and three different services, you've gotta have some place to safely direct the incoming and outgoing stampede.

At first I suspected Janine's quick maneuverings were to avoid the coming very public verbal flogging by one Mrs. De'Laruse due to our tardiness. But when I saw the shock of blond hovering above the cookie crowd, I knew the ulterior motive wasn't for her benefit.

I wish I was as thoughtful as my bestie.

The passage of eleven years had been oh so very kind to Bobby – I mean, Pastor Bobby. Pastor Robert Vernet.

The tall scrawny star of the Christian Bible Fellowship High School's state championship basketball team had grown nicely into his six-foot-six frame. Broad man-shoulders towered over most, his smile lighting up the room like the star on top of a Christmas tree.

And that's considering a Texas-sized tree like my mom always liked.

Bobby definitely had Texas-sized down pat – in every way imaginable. Believe me. Visions of F-150s danced in my hell-bent head.

"You wanna bib?" Janine asked, disrupting my precious memories.

"Huh?"

"You know, to soak up all that drool."

Lord, I was going straight to Hell. Here I'd come all this way to make amends for the past, and all I wanted to do right then was repeat it. Bad girl. Bad, bad...

"Vicki!"

"What?"

"You're in church, remember?" Janine reminded.

"Right," I muttered.

In church, surrounded by the gossiping gaggle, members of the pastoral staff, and my first summer fling – who was now a pastor as well.

Married.

Had a child on the way.

I mentally slapped myself and followed the welcoming committee forward toward the prize.

I mean pastor. Followed them toward the pastor.

Janine snickered like she had a front row seat to my mental musings and rolled her eyes. I gave her my best evil eye and got my ribs poked in the process.

"My, my, my. Who do we have here?"

It didn't require turning around to recognize that voice. It sent chalkboard chills down my spine and got my hackles up before Janine could say *bitch-alert*.

Kansas has the Wicked Witch of the West. Texas has Lorraine Padget, all five-foot ten-inches – counting her hair anyway – of a former Miss Texas runner-up who clawed her way under the crown when some scandalous pictures and videos involving the original winner came to light.

In some parts, that would've thrust the real winner to instant stardom. Here in the south though, we still want our beauty queens to be prim, proper, and pure.

Or in Lorraine's case to at least have the smarts not to get caught with photographic evidence.

Did I mention she was also the on-again-off-again high school girlfriend of one Bobby Vernet? AKA the senior pastor's kid. AKA the new children's pastor. AKA my virginity stealer.

Though it's a well-documented fact I gave it away willingly.

After her half-year stint as the Miss Texas title holder – albeit too late for the Miss America pageant, thank God – Lorraine went on to become a journalist. With her newfound notoriety, she slept her way into a local co-anchor position and recently landed an old, but rich, fish.

All techniques learned from her mother, I imagine.

She was also the daughter of one of my dad's many conquests. Yup, Saturday night sleepovers with Lisa.

"Lorraine Padget," I said, turning around and pasting on a matching too big grin.

"As I live and breathe." The plaster coating of makeup on Lorraine's face threatened to splinter and crack around the Botox smile. "I always had faith you'd leave behind your harlotry ways and return to the fold. Glory hallelujah!"

Takes one to know one, but I wasn't about to give Lorraine the pleasure of acknowledging the harlotry comment.

"Just here to say hi to an old friend," I said before smiling at her somewhat familiar companion. "Care to make introductions?"

The pious Padget shot me a glare before remembering the baggage on her arm. The guy looked like he'd never survive to Christmas, though I had to give the white-haired codger another ten years benefit of the doubt – if only to see Lorraine suffer. The rock she flashed almost blinded me.

"My manners," Lorraine said, tilting her hand to make sure I got a good look at the stone. "Sweetheart, this is my dear friend from high school days, Miss Victoria Bohanan. Victoria, meet my fiancé, Mr. Derek Summers."

"Bohanan?" Mr. Summers wheezed. "Frank's girl?"

I gripped the bony and weathered hand. "How do you do, Mr. Summers? Yes, Frank Bohanan's daughter, if he still claims me that is."

That earned me a cackle, though I was afraid the pronounced cough might send him into cardiac arrest. Lorraine gathered him up to get him a drink, though I suspected Mr. Summers went for something a little stronger than water with that bulbous red nose.

Most oilmen of that generation always did. Any generation really. It gave them something to talk about besides the price of crude.

When I turned around, my panties nearly dropped where I stood. Bobby Vernet's smile stilled my heart.

His voice jumpstarted it again. "Hello, Vicki."

The entire room fell into a hushed silence and all motion stopped. Every eye on three levels darted toward our little reunion.

Or maybe that was just my imagination.

For a moment, I almost expected the Heavenly Host to break out into the Hallelujah Chorus – which would then shatter the glass enclosure and send a shower of shards right into my backslidden carcass.

"Hey, Bobby."

All five-foot-six of me was enveloped by all six-foot-six of him. Lord Almighty, help me breathe. A different scent than what I remembered wafted from his skin. Probably something the wife liked better.

The wife!

Sound stirred as I pulled from the embrace to stare at the diminutive woman by Bobby's side. Long brown curls surrounded a rounded face and dark eyes that sparkled with amusement. All five-foot-nothing was swathed in a lavender chiffon dress that revealed a small protrusion at the belly.

She beamed as she grasped my hands. If it weren't for the glow of pregnancy, I'd say the smile appeared genuine.

"Vicki," Bobby said, "I'd like you to meet my wife, Amy."

"I'm so pleased to finally meet you," Amy gushed.

A singer's voice. She and Janine would get on great. The little green-eyed monster of envy threatened to climb on my back before I shook it off.

"Finally?" I questioned.

"Rob has told me so much about you. And this must be Janine."

Amy vigorously grasped Janine's hands after releasing mine. My best friend shot me a side glance as they engaged in brief conversation. What could Bobby have possibly said to this woman to make her so eager to meet us?

"So it's Rob now?"

Bobby chuckled. "Sounds a little more grown up than Bobby, don't you think?"

I had to laugh. "Just don't trade the car for a van yet."

"Vans offer a little more leg room, but not as much as trucks, am I right?"

Was it getting hot in here, or was it just me?

Bobby handed me a card. "Give me a call if you're free sometime this week. It'd be good to catch up."

Did he just...? In front of...? What the...?

I couldn't remember the last time something – *anything* – had made me blush.

Guess there's a first time for everything.

CHAPTER SIX

Inside or outside? That was the question.

Most quaint bistros in the Dallas area offered two choices of seating, each with their own benefits and drawbacks. Inside offered dark corners, protection for those who wished to carry on quiet conversation and hide intimate gestures.

The downside for me? Temptation waiting to happen or innocent actions misconstrued.

Choosing the table along the sidewalk for Thursday's luncheon would keep things above board. But it was also June in Texas. Heat and humidity combined to make life for any normal person miserable.

Plus, Thursdays were also the church ladies luncheon. As the newest pastoral member of the congregation, Amy would be the headliner at this week's gathering. With the close proximity of the bistro to the church, tongues would wag faster than a dog's tail at dinnertime if the wrong people drove by and saw me and Bobby alone together.

I sighed. No matter which seating location I chose, we'd still be screwed – er, uh, befouled – uh...

Oh hell.

I just didn't want to do anything to sully Bobby's rehabilitated reputation. Eenie-meenie-miney-mo. The outdoor table won the coin toss.

Call me surprised when Amy showed up on Bobby's arm instead of attending the church luncheon. Those tongue waggers if they saw us? Out of luck today.

I leapt from my chair to greet them in relief. "Hey, all."

"Vicki, I'm so glad to have this chance to talk," Amy said as she grappled me in a hug. The womb-bound baby fist-bumped my hip. "Oh. He's been pretty active today. Looking forward to lunch as much as I am."

Bobby pulled out a chair for Amy then leaned over and pecked me on the cheek before taking a seat. The physical contact sent a zing to my heart, and it literally skipped a beat.

"So it's a boy, is it?" I questioned as I returned to my wicker chair.

Bobby beamed like a proud soon-to-be dad. "Yep, and I'm looking forward to a game of one-on-one already."

"Rob," Amy playfully chastised, "we already agreed he'd choose his own sport."

"That's only because you want him to play football."

"We *are* in Texas, remember?"

"Yeah, *Rob*," I interjected and scooted my chair a little closer to Amy. "What's up with that?"

Bobby glanced between us like a man who'd been double-teamed. Amy and I batted our lashes and stared expectantly, waiting for an answer. I'd barely met this woman, and already we'd sided together over football.

At this rate, I could really like Amy if I tried.

"Uh-oh," Bobby said. "I knew introducing an old girlfriend to my wife was a mistake."

Those chummy feelings I'd just had? Yeah, they disappeared right quick. Let the earth erupt and consume me on the spot.

"You told her?" I redirected my embarrassment toward Amy. "He told you we went out?"

Like a calm and collected pastor's wife, Amy patted my hand. "It's okay. Rob and I wanted no secrets between us when we married. No skeletons that would come bursting from the closet."

"But not…" I hesitated as I glanced Bobby's way.

A tinge of color popped into Bobby's cheeks. "It's safe to say that was never a secret after the police showed up."

Lord, take me now! To purgatory if the Catholics are right. Just don't send me to Hell. I'm already there.

No secrets? A marriage with no skeletons? Were these two serious? A couple actually communicating within a marriage was a foreign concept.

My father had to be the king of closeted skeletons – or at least he tried to keep them in there. Bound, gagged, and encased in cement shoes. Any Mafia boss would do well to practice his techniques.

Amy wrapped her arm around my shoulders. "Would it help to know I too was a wilted flower before I met my husband?"

Wilted flower? Had this woman learned her vocabulary from my mother?

"Maybe by tomorrow it will," I muttered.

'Cept I was no wilted flower. Plucked to the stem better described me.

I was so looking forward to work tonight. I was gonna get shit-faced. Plastered on the boss's dime. Maybe even get laid.

No! That kind of thinking was what had gotten me here in the first place. What had happened to my resolve to clean up my act? Lay off the getting laid?

Oh yeah. Nick had happened. Then Nick happened again. And again. Yummy goodness all wrapped up in rock hard abs, rock hard butt, and rock hard…

Victoria!

Sometimes I conjured up Mom's voice in my head. Her good shoulder angel to my bad. Rarely worked for me either.

"So," I said in a desperate attempt to steer the conversation along a new path. "What made you guys decide to come home, and why now?"

"We always planned to return," Bobby explained. "It just took a little convincing to move earlier than scheduled when the children's pastorate opened up."

"Sometimes God's plans are on a different timetable than our own," Amy offered.

The clatter of breaking glasses and an angry shout from a nearby patron interrupted my mental musings. A stream of Spanish erupted from the embarrassed waitress as she stooped to pick up shards and sop up the mess from the disgruntled man's lunch.

Moving faster than what I thought possible for a pregnant woman, Amy slipped from her chair to assist. The rapidity of her words matched the distressed waitress's and the situation was soothed before Bobby unfolded himself from our table to help Amy back into her chair.

"Where are you originally from, Amy?" I asked.

A shadow momentarily clouded the perpetual sparkle in her eyes. "Brownsville. Some of my extended family is still there."

I smiled. "You can take the girl out of Texas, but you can't take Texas out of the girl."

Amy laughed and the glimmer of joy returned. "Something like that."

The roundtable embarrassment evaporated nearly as fast as rain in the desert. As lunch progressed, I found Amy to be a surprising breath of fresh air within the community of pious purveyors I'd grown up with. She spoke of her own past shortcomings in a nonchalant manner and explained that since she'd been forgiven her mountain of sins, she could in turn forgive the sins of others.

Her demeanor reflected a peace I'd rarely seen among the Holy Huddlers. Surrounded by those people, would Amy eventually succumb to their ways?

Something assured me she wouldn't.

I looked forward to knowing Amy better. For the first time I felt comfortable around someone of the saintly persuasion. Maybe because Amy didn't put on airs.

Didn't act arrogant and better than others with a chip on her shoulder any cow would be proud of.

Didn't speak about others with contempt that had her nose up so high she'd drown in a rainstorm.

Didn't act like the favorited chosen of the frozen. Amy, I was surprised to realize, was the real thing.

Yeah, me thinks I could really like this Brownsville transplant.

Thursday night shenanigans had ramped up to a frenzy by the time my co-worker showed his mug. The summertime wet t-shirt opener might've had a little something to do with the rowdiness too.

Ah – gotta love summer.

Grady left bartending duty and launched onto the platform to make announcements amid a backdrop of heavy black plastic sheeting. The usual ethereal theme of the dance floor had been removed to transform the space into more of a countrified jamboree – appropriate for the night's festivities.

Girls of all ages, shapes, and cup sizes congregated together onstage to a chorus of wolf whistles and cat calls.

"Hey, Bud. Nice of you to show up," I yelled, slinging drinks out at the hooting patrons faster than charges add up on my mother's credit card.

"Anytime, sweet cheeks," he returned.

Bud – so not his real name. Probably had an uppity name like Bradley to match the underlying northern accent. Most accepted the Texas twang, as fake as his blond hair, but I could detect it as sure as I could hit a target from a hundred feet. Maybe fifty.

Okay, so it's more like twenty-five, so sue me.

Not sure where Bud came up with the moniker, but I'm pretty sure it had something to do with seeing a bottle of Budweiser upon entering the great State of Texas. Since then, *this Bud's for you* took on a whole new meaning when asking women what they'd have.

At least in his mind.

Slobbery lips trickled down my neck as Bud sidled up behind me, wrapped a meat hook around my midriff, and pressed against my daisy dukes. In a flash, I dropped the bottle of rum on the counter and reached behind to grip a handful of jean.

The high-pitched squeak heard 'round the bar told me I'd nabbed just the right spot. Bud didn't so much as breathe.

"How many times do I have to tell you, this Bud ain't for me?" I growled. "So kindly remove your slimy lips before *I* do the twist and *you* shout."

That got a chuckle out of Rochelle as she dropped off a tray of dirty glasses, rinsed them out and started filling up the dishwasher.

See? I don't just crack myself up.

When Bud's lips released my neck, I relinquished my claim on his family jewels. Someone get me some bleach – stat.

"Damn, girl." Bud rearranged himself in front of God and the entire club. "You let Grady and any guy here gnaw on you all night long. What gives?"

"First," I said, holding up a single finger – no, not that one. "It isn't just any guy here. Second, they've all got something you lack."

"You ain't never heard no complaints from the girls I've been with."

I whirled around. Bud flinched. "I'm talking a little C-L-A-S-S. Emphasis on the C and L and less on the piece of ASS."

The rust on the wheels of Bud's brain broke loose as he scrunched up his face and so obviously struggled to place the letters together to form a word.

I think he gave up.

"So what's got you all riled up tonight, Vicki?"

"For starters, how about you dragging your sorry ass in here over two hours late? Not to mention you still smell like shit."

I poured a little rum into a patron's drink and dropped in an umbrella before sloshing it onto the bar and taking a queen-sized swig for myself.

The hooting and hollering near the stage reached epic proportions as Grady hosed down a particularly busty brunette. Talk about fake. The girl could use those puppies as floatation devices instead of the seat cushion in an airplane water landing.

Rochelle and I exchanged knowing eye rolls. I poured her a shot then tossed back another swig of rum. It was setting up to be one of those nights where I'd need all the libations I could swallow.

"I have other obligations, you know," Bud said.

"Couldn't get it up?" Rochelle asked.

That earned her a sideways glare while Bud scooped ice into a glass. "My other *job*. Cattle ain't gonna herd themselves, ladies."

"You sure you ain't talkin' a *blow* job?" I slurred and filled up a line of mugs from the tap.

"Hey, I'm doing you a favor even being here tonight, what with Wanker out of town. Don't know why Grady didn't get Baby in here with you instead."

"Cause she'd be up on stage working the crowd instead of working the bar," Rochelle explained, balancing the tray of freshly dispensed beer and heading back into the wild horde.

After gulping down my second Long Island iced tea amid all the other assorted sips and slurps, hell *I* was hardly working the bar. By the time the contest whittled down to the final five contestants, I'd finished lining the front of the counter with watered-down beer pitchers.

I tied my barely-there t-shirt in a knot just below my boobs, shoved my cell phone underneath the counter, then climbed atop my perch. My high-pitched whistle rattled through my pickled brain, and the patron fight over pitchers was on.

Buy me a drink – or two or three – and I can come up with some fun ways to create a diversion. The distracting dousing took all of ten seconds away from the main attraction before the pitchers were all emptied on little ol' me. Pretty sure a few got guzzled instead of thrown my direction – some people will drink anything as long as it's free.

At Grady's call, someone swept me off the bar top, and I hefted the trophy to the stage to present to the champion in all my perky glory.

Fake Boobs ended up the winner. I was satisfied knowing mine were God-given instead of physician-provided. The whistles and appreciative stares redirected my way said Fake Boobs may have taken home the trophy, but I was the real winner in the crowd's eyes – all hundred and something lusty, testosterone-fueled eyes.

If I wanted, I could have my pick tonight. Really any night. But even through my alcohol-induced haze, I remembered my pledge to lay off the getting laid. This was gonna be harder – er, more difficult than I'd thought.

Thank God Nick hadn't shown up tonight.

Cleaning up after wet t-shirt night was never as much fun as the event itself. By the time I finished counting the till, my shirt had mostly dried but my daisy dukes were still a bit gooey and hiked so far up my butt I'd need surgery to remove them. My Tony Lamas would never again be the same.

My somewhat inebriated state had cleared during clean-up faster than Bud had disappeared. Last to arrive. First to leave.

Figured.

I waved to Rochelle and watched out the backdoor until she safely drove off into the muggy night, then lugged the important things to the backroom.

"Bud skipped out on clean-up again," I grumbled to Grady as I entered the office and plunked the cash box on his desk.

The array of security camera feeds flashed across the screens and revealed the inside of the bar from every angle, as well as the parking lot of not only Grady's but the surrounding clubs too.

My boss took security about as seriously as the guys did at Fort Knox. I always assumed it was carryover from his military stint.

After he closed his laptop, I handed over the inventory tally sheets and a scrap of paper with my nightly tab total. Grady barely glanced at the scrap before wadding up it and tossing it in the trash.

He shook his head as he locked up the safe and grabbed his hat along with a black plastic bag. "I told ya a long time ago, ya don't have to keep a tab anymore."

I shrugged. "I know. But I figure this way it keeps me honest."

"Since I hired ya, business has nearly doubled." Grady locked the metal office door behind us and keyed in the alarm code. "What your antics bring in more than make up for what ya cost me in drinks."

"Okay, fine. But what are you gonna do about Bud?" I asked as we exited the building and walked across the lot to my car.

"He stayed for a good portion of clean-up this time," Grady said.

"Barely," I returned. "And two hours late again. Why have you kept his lazy carcass around so long? It isn't like I can't handle the bar by myself."

Grady shrugged. "Favor to an old Army buddy, I suppose."

"What'd this Army buddy do? Save your life or something like that?" I asked as I dug my car keys out of my gooey pocket. "Cause if not, then you're getting the short end of the bargain."

"Favors among brothers-in-arms never come cheap," he said, opening my driver's side door after the beep. "Bud's his younger brother."

"Oh," was all I could muster.

"Ya smell like stale beer," Grady observed.

"Thanks to you I'm wearing makeup down to my ankles too."

"Cain't tell me ya didn't enjoy the attention."

I smiled. "It was kinda fun participating this year."

"Technically ya cain't win though."

"I know."

"Here's some plastic to put on your car seat," Grady offered as he pressed a kiss to my forehead. "Sure you're okay to drive?"

"More than okay," I said breathlessly.

"Yes. Yes, you are."

Grady's chocolate depths made my knees go all noodley again. The back of his hand brushed against a perky protrusion when he brought the plastic bag between us.

I shivered from the cool night air, though Dallas nights rarely dropped below eighty-five degrees in summer. Tonight must be one of the rarelys.

Or at least that was my story.

"See ya tomorrow night," Grady's husky voice called as he sauntered away to his sleek black Dodge Ram.

After I tore my eyes away from the boss, the plastic trash bag slid right over the driver's seat of my Vette almost as if tailor made. Grady always took special care of me.

No, not in that way, no matter how much the image of the plastic sheath sliding over my seat reminded me of a condom. I was determined to keep business separate from pleasure.

"Where were you last Saturday night?"

The question was tinged with an Aussie accent. My entire body jerked so hard my head smacked against the doorframe of my car and shattered the naughty images of me and the boss floating around my mind.

Nick's perfectly mussed hair topped off his perfectly chiseled face set upon a perfectly pumped-up body. The perfectly hung silk shirt opened a little too perfectly for my present sanity.

"What the hell, Nick?" I asked as I stood up. "You tryin' to scare me half to death or just crack my skull open?"

The fragrance saturating his chest wafted my way on the breeze and touched me all the way down there. Cologne he likely got from one of his modeling gigs. Earthy. Expensive. Erotic.

"I missed you," Nick said as he brushed hair from my face and pressed in closer.

I could feel how much he'd missed me. That and the accent curled my toes so tight I thought my boots would come flying off.

He massaged the base of my skull where a knot formed. I swallowed the one forming in my throat and reminded myself of my vow.

Didn't the Bible say something about resisting the devil and he'd flee? How many guys did a girl have to chase away in one night before temptation fled?

"Yeah?" My voice trembled. "I-uh, took the night off. Where were you earlier this week?"

"Work."

Velvety little kisses trailed across my forehead where Grady's lips had rested moments before.

"You taste like old beer," Nick said, his tongue flicking in and out all the way down to my jaw.

"Things got a little out of hand during wet t-shirt night."

"Mmm. Did you win?"

"I technically wasn't a participant."

Smooth and tanned pectorals beckoned. Can you say reach out and touch someone? I can.

And did.

"Why didn't you call me?" Nick asked, sucking in a sharp breath as my fingertips feathered his six pack.

I thought girls were supposed to be the needy ones? Questions dissipated as Nick dipped to my ear and nuzzled the lobe between his teeth. Gooseflesh raced across the surface of my skin. My spine turned to pudding.

"Um, Nick?"

"Hmm?"

"Maybe you should slow down there. This is a public parking lot."

A button popped and skittered somewhere along the pavement as my wandering hands edged deeper into his shirt. Warm lips suckled my neck where my pulse throbbed until plunging to graze between my twin peaks.

A moan escaped from one of us as he pressed against me so hard I slid up and onto the hood of the Vette until I was practically lying on top of it.

So much for resisting temptation.

Headlights and blinding spotlights atop the roll bar cut through the dimmed parking lot and brought Nick's face up to mine. I pushed him away and shimmied down when Grady pulled his truck alongside, rolled down the window, and leaned out.

The crooked tilt of his mustache said he'd enjoyed our little show. "You alright there, Vic?"

I straightened and adjusted myself, tucking a sticky strand of hair behind my ear. Any chance of getting my shorts out of my butt without surgery was a lost cause now.

"I'm fine. All's good. You can go home now."

Grady offered a two-fingered salute before rolling up his window. The creeping crawl of his truck said he wasn't leaving until I was safe in my car.

The reprieve from temptation and self-condemning acts was handed to me on a silver platter from above – or from a black Dodge driven by my boss.

I patted Nick's arm, leaned in and kissed him on the cheek. "Maybe next time, mate."

All I got in return was a husky and frustrated sigh.

I hopped in my car, revved the engine of my little black Corvette then laid down a few skid marks, leaving Nick behind in my dust. Reprieve indeed.

Unfortunately it'd take a lot more to untangle the numerous men from my life. Why'd everything have to be so complicated?

When I rounded the corner from my apartment building to a chorus of police sirens and a blaze of blue and red strobe lights, I realized *my* life wasn't so complicated after all.

CHAPTER SEVEN

If you would've told me on Sunday I'd be attending church twice in one week, I'd have laughed and patted your cheek like Grandma used to do when I said something to amuse her.

The only reason I'd gone Sunday was to see what had become of Bobby in his decade-long absence since, as a pastor, it was doubtful he'd ever set foot in my present circle. Therefore, I'd had to suck it up – no pun intended – and step up to his.

A funeral, however, was no laughing matter.

Janine's a crier and goes through more tissues during a romance movie than we stuffed in our training bras throughout fourth grade. My blouse became her secondary snot rag while I sat in stunned silence as Pastor Dennis's eulogy droned on like a steadily ticking metronome, swiping sweat and tears in tandem.

Not sure how he rattled through it all – considering.

I'd looked forward to reacquainting myself with Bobby and establishing a friendship with Amy. She'd seemed so open to becoming friends and had accepted me right where I was, unlike the rest of the holier-than-thou crowd.

But for someone who, for all intents and purposes, appeared so content with life, why'd she commit suicide?

And why do it by throwing herself off a building?

Next burning question – what was she doing on *my* rooftop?

How could I have been so wrong about her? The death of a spouse was bad enough, but snuffing out the life of their unborn son angered me more than a whiskey shortage on a Saturday. Amy's actions were the epitome of selfishness. Not just one life lost, but two.

I'm not sure how Bobby got through the emotional and high-strung service. If it'd been me in his shoes, you'd have had to load me up on valium and a good dose of liquor to even drag me out of the house.

Yes, I know drugs and alcohol don't mix. I'm simply trying to make a point here. Work with me, folks.

When the church service ended with a final choked amen, like a trail of worker ants we all dutifully followed one another out of the sanctuary and behind the hearse to the gravesite. The line of cars had gawkers entertained for miles and impatient drivers cursing the interruption to their Saturday shopping excursions.

As torn up as my best friend was, I'd have never thought Janine had it in her to buck the family and ride with me. I couldn't even make out half of what she wailed between sobs and snorts, but I nodded and offered an occasional mmm-hmm until we parked.

Now don't get me wrong. I'm not a cold-hearted bitch.

Long ago I'd learned that public displays of emotion rarely served any other purpose than to give your enemy a peek at your weaknesses. Provided ammunition for their next attack. It was a lesson I'd learned the hard way.

But once I was alone again at my apartment, all bets were off.

Since Pastor Dennis was tight with my dad – or at least with his checkbook – our family was afforded graveside seating with the Vernets. Mom sat in the middle, keeping me separated from the other half of my chromosomal donor.

It was then I got more than a glimpse of Bobby's red-rimmed eyes and the shell-shocked slack of his jaw. Dark circles spoke volumes of how little sleep – if any – he'd had over the last couple of days.

A dull ache clenched my heart in its fist as we stared at not just one coffin but two, the small honorary blue one for the tiny life taken too soon.

That seemed almost cruel. Whose decision was it to have this second coffin? Whoever it was, they may as well have just burrowed the knife deeper into Bobby's heart right there in front of everyone.

A furtive glance at the familiar faces around us struck me with a curiosity. What about Amy's family? It was her funeral after all.

Where were those who claimed DNA with the deceased? The woman who had warmed the Amy bun in her womb for nine months? The man who'd submitted a stray chromosomal strand?

Grandparents?

Siblings?

Strange they were all absent.

At lunch the other day, I'd never asked Amy about her side of the family, and she'd never volunteered any information. There was only the brief exchange about being from Brownsville.

Was I really that self-absorbed to have failed to pry into someone else's genealogical history?

Apparently so.

The post-funeral meal was held at the Vernet family estate, a mansion dedicated to spreading their version of the gospel, which in Dennis and Mary Jo's book was centered on money and how to gain more of it.

Personally, I thought the mansion built for two reflected more fleecing of the flock than anything remotely resembling the Man they publicly claimed to emulate.

Security at the gate to enter the Vernet domain was tighter than that at Fort Knox. People were turned away left and right in a constant stream. If it wasn't for the fact that I drove right behind my parents and carried the last name of *Bohanan*, I doubt I'd have been allowed through.

'Course it didn't hurt either that a De'Laruse sat in the passenger's seat of my Corvette.

Even with a caterer, Mary Jo buzzed from ginormous over-decorated room to ginormous overstuffed room, playing the perfect hostess and ensuring all had their fill from the massive spread.

Staying in motion also kept her from holding still long enough to allow food to touch her lips. The woman was as stick thin as her husband was round.

Rumor had it Mary Jo enjoyed a nip and tuck on occasion to stave off encroaching middle-age sag.

Though we all know by now that I'm not one to listen to the rumor mill.

The painted smile, however, was a permanent fixture and bespoke work more along the lines of the Botox variety. Or maybe silicone.

Made her look less like a real woman and more like the Joker. You know, from Batman. The garish grin appeared odd and definitely out of place, considering the somber events surrounding her son.

Bobby held up the Italian marble mantelpiece in the formal living room all afternoon, receiving an endless parade of condolences. From the blank stare and robot-like movement of shaking hands, I rather think the mantelpiece held *him* up.

No matter how much I wanted to wrap my arms around and comfort one of my oldest friends, I kept my distance. Not for my sake, mind you. I'd long ago stopped caring what the sanctified saints thought of me.

But I did care about what it might do to Bobby's reputation and how it would affect his position at the church to be seen in the arms of this unholy hell raiser once again. It might spur memories in others better left to my gray matter.

Like of F-150s that go *vroom*.

His life didn't need any further complications. And in his present state, I doubt if he'd even remember who was and wasn't at his wife's funeral.

The fact that I even felt the need to keep my distance churned up more stomach acid than my internal debate over choice of tables had at the bistro Thursday afternoon.

'Course the stares and fake smiles of the crowd as they whispered behind my back didn't help either. They were like vultures waiting to swoop down on fresh road kill. As far as I was concerned they could all starve to death before I'd give them that satisfaction.

Mary Jo brought Bobby yet another full plate of food, which he held in front of himself as if establishing a perimeter to avoid those pressing in around him. Eventually he gave up and set it untouched behind him on the hearth.

One of the four Vernet Corgis had picked up on his actions early on, staying close for the next available plate. The feet of those canine sausage rolls wouldn't touch the ground by the end of the day if the meals kept coming.

"Hello, daughter."

Speaking of dogs...

"Hey, Frankie. How's life?"

Finally! Someone I could take out the day's frustrations on.

Grandma always had a thing for Frankie Avalon in her younger years. The affection was so strong, she named her son after the famous crooner. Too bad my dad didn't have the head of hair left to match, though pictures from his younger days at least showed me where I'd gotten the dark hair.

These days he looked more like Daddy Warbucks. Or Lex Luther – with the attitude to match.

Most people now called him by the more respectable *Frank*, though my use of the childhood namesake was less from affection and more for barb launching. The riling never got old.

At least not for me.

The sperm donor's face remained placid, but the infinitesimal narrowing of the eyelids told me I'd hit the intended mark with the moniker. The pinched thinning of Mom's lips gave me a moment's pause though.

But just a moment.

"Your mother and I are leaving," Frank said, "as I have some important work related calls to return."

Work my ass. Work on one Lisa Padget, no doubt. The man couldn't even take one day away from rooting around for business.

Or in this case, rooting around *in* someone's business.

"Enjoy your work then."

"Don't you think it's time you left as well?"

"I've got my own car. I'll leave when I'm ready."

All that got me was the *look*.

Come on, you know what I'm saying. That look signifying displeasure at whatever transgression you committed this time. Real or imaginary.

Growing up I'd been subjected to it so many times I'd lost count, and its effectiveness had diminished. Nowadays I simply ignored it. I was no longer a slave to his whims. Making my own way in the world brought freedom.

"Don't worry, Frankie," I continued, lowering my voice so the nearby predators couldn't hear. "I've no plans to embarrass you. Even if I wanted to, your leaving would only deny you the pleasure of appreciating the full effect."

My mother leaned in and pecked me on the cheek before whispering in my ear. "Play nice."

Frank shook his head. "Must you always try to cause a scene?"

"Hey, don't I get credit for trying *not* to?"

A kiss in return for my mom accompanied by a Cheshire cat grin for the sperm donor, then my mom steered them toward the exit. The moment they stepped from the house, I breathed a sigh of relief.

Being in the same building – hell, the same city sometimes – as my father brought on tension thicker than an Angus beef steak.

The vultures soon tired of waiting for a public spectacle, involving me and Bobby in close proximity, and thinned from the premises. I was sorry to see Janine go, but she was marched out the door with the rest of the De'Laruse clan soon after my parents.

I considered offering her another ride, but at this point I figured she was in enough trouble for riding with me earlier. Plus, with so many leaving at once, Bobby needed my presence more than Janine needed rescuing.

When the majority of the herd had made their way past the foyer, Bobby sagged to a blue chintz sofa. The time was as good as any, so I took a chance, sat down beside him and offered a hug.

I felt rather than heard the collective gasp from stragglers. Let them think what they wanted at this point. I was beyond caring anymore.

"Thanks for coming, Vic." Bobby's voice quivered. "It means a lot to me that you're here."

My throat constricted to hear him call me by the pet name. Only a handful of close friends had ever called me that, Bobby being the first. The first of so many things.

All I squeaked out in response was, "I'm so sorry, Bobby."

The avalanche shifted. Then it melted and tore down the mountain all at once. After holding back all day, Bobby finally broke down in my arms.

I didn't care about tears and snot on my silk blouse – Janine had already gotten to it.

I didn't care about the stares and pictures snapped and uploaded to social media or the tongue wagging that ensued.

All I cared about was comforting my devastated friend.

"You wanna get away from this for a spell?" I asked.

Bobby just nodded.

I grabbed the keys from my clutch as we stood. Then we walked through the crowd that parted before us like the Red Sea and strode out the front door.

The unlocking beep of the Vette echoed loudly in the stunned silence as we got in my car and drove away before the rest of the Vernet family could raise any objection.

The gossiping gaggle could kiss my lily-white ass.

CHAPTER EIGHT

Years ago when Bobby and I would get together to talk – yes, we did that too – we always made sure to finish off the six-pack and get a good buzz going before he'd drop me near the family gates to sneak into the house.

About the only buzz I'd get tonight would be when the need to pee hit. I always could hold my liquor better than my soda pop.

The wind slaked through the pasture grass, carrying with it the faint scent of manure, while cows lowed in the distance. My little car didn't handle washboard dirt roads very well, but the need to get away from crowds trumped the need to protect my prized possession. Friends held more value than stuff.

At least for me.

After finishing off a second can and crunching it in his hands, Bobby broke the silence. "I owe you a long overdue apology."

"For what?" I asked before taking a swig of cola.

"For what happened eleven years ago."

I stifled the memories of that F-150. So not the time. So inappropriate in this situation.

'Specially because that's what the remaining company of backstabbing believers back at the Vernet mansion probably thought when we'd left together.

"Wasn't like I was an unwilling participant or anything," I admitted.

Bobby took a deep breath. "But then I went away to college, leaving you to face the wrath alone."

"I survived."

"I was a coward who ran off with my tail between my legs."

"Well, I wouldn't call it a tail exactly."

His head jerked my direction so fast, I thought Bobby would end up with whiplash. The whole countryside sucked in a collective gasp and held it until laughter burst from his lips.

It was good to hear the deep and rumbling guffaw. Lord knows there'd been little to be jovial about the last few days.

"Did you know," I continued, "that my father even considered bringing statutory rape charges against you?"

That shut him up right quick. "You serious?"

I nodded. "But that threat dissipated pretty quick after I reminded him about a certain stack of photos."

My opinion of the sperm donor reached its how-low-can-you-go, point-of-no-return just before my fourteenth birthday. The envelope of pictures I'd discovered beneath a loose plank in the attic of the Galveston family vacation home soon taught me the real meaning of the phrase *business trip*.

In private my father had always treated me and my mom with unveiled contempt like the heartless bastard he was. But that day I learned the graphic truth about his secret life.

And the power of a named and dated Polaroid.

"Still using blackmail against the old man, are we?" Bobby asked.

"Nah. Moving out on my own works better...for both of us. Keeps at bay the possibility of the cops cleaning up a double homicide."

We both flinched.

See, there's this disease I have commonly known around these parts as foot-in-mouth disease. My taste for shoe leather and toe jam hadn't improved with time or age.

"Poor choice of words," I said. "I'm so sorry."

Warmth enveloped my hand as his covered mine. "It's okay, Vicki."

Now it was my turn to choke up as Bobby held my hand and laid back against the windshield to stare into the sky. The Corvette hood didn't hold us as well as his truck bed had, but it didn't stop us from again sharing the wonder of watching the horizon turn from yellow to orange, then pink to periwinkle.

The only place you could really enjoy the expanse of a Texas sunset was outside the metropolis that was Dallas. Tonight we'd had to drive a lot farther than we used to in order to escape the suburban sprawl.

A deep sigh before Bobby interrupted the opening strains of the cricket chorus. "This is what I missed most about Texas."

"The sunsets?"

"Mm-hmm. The sky just goes on and on forever." His voice dropped off for a bit. "It's been so busy since we arrived, I never got to share this with Amy." Emotion choked his words. "I'll never share this with my son."

Silent tears streaked his face before the growing darkness swathed him in shadows. Anger boiled me anew.

Even with our checkered past, Bobby had always been the friend to me Janine couldn't. Janine was too sweet. Wanted too much to please. When we were all growing up, I understood the pressures Bobby faced, and he mine.

Being a preacher's kid, Bobby had to play a part like an actor for the masses, all the while knowing what went on behind the scenes of a massive and bloated religious enterprise.

He knew about the battle sequences between his dad and the church leadership, my father being one of the battle instigators.

He'd witnessed and heard things even I hadn't. And I'd known a lot, at least with what pertained to my own family.

Our friendship had started because of our mutual family involvements, and over the years the commiseration had kept us somewhat sane.

At least until our well-publicized hook-up.

"It's my fault, you know," Bobby whispered.

"What is?"

"That they're dead."

That bolted me upright. "Well 'scuse my French, pastor, but that's a load of shit. No, not just a load, but a heaping helping *ass*-load of *bull*-shit." I waved my hand around. "Just sniff the air."

That earned me a caffeinated belch and a shake of the head. "You always were the more eloquent of the two of us."

I shrugged. "I try."

"You know, Amy wasn't ready to move back to Texas," Bobby confessed. "But then she got pregnant. The children's ministry job opened up and all. It was like God had placed a giant, neon arrow in the sky pointing us here. I even told her that."

Stomach acid churning started all over again. Maybe it was too much carbonated pop, even though a loud burp didn't ease it.

"I can't stand this anymore." I chucked my can into the weeds. "Doesn't it piss you off at all?"

Bobby stared into his cola can before launching it to join mine with an ease that bespoke his basketball prowess. "I'm not angry with anyone but myself, Vic. Why would I be?"

Flies could've camped in my mouth. "Your wife committed suicide! While she was pregnant. I mean, she basically murdered your son, Bobby."

There went my disease-ridden mouth again.

"She didn't commit suicide," he whispered.

That shut me up – for all of two seconds. "Come again?"

Between the deepening shadows, for the first time since Bobby's life went sideways, I saw anger reflected in the depths of his eyes.

"Amy did *not* commit suicide. Regardless of what the police say, I'm as sure as the second coming that my wife did not jump off your building of her own accord."

Maybe the head jerk earlier *had* caused whiplash. Oxygen and blood no longer seemed to be making its way toward Bobby's gray matter.

"I don't know about the second coming, but do I need to call the men in white?" I asked.

The Vette shook as Bobby shoved off and paced a cattle trail through the nearby pasture grass. Some things never changed.

It's a wonder he'd been able to hold still all afternoon by the fireplace, though I imagine during that time he'd been trying *not* to think.

"There are things about Amy's past she never got to share with you," Bobby finally admitted. "Things about her family connections."

"Why would she share with me?"

"I don't know...some spiritual connection she felt with you when we aired our dirty laundry the other day."

A spiritual connection? Truth be told, I'd rather felt it as well. But I wasn't ready yet to acknowledge some sort of inner-workings of the cosmos.

"Does this have something to do with them not attending her funeral?" I asked.

"You noticed that too?"

"You know me. I notice everything. It's a curse."

Bobby stopped pacing and stared at the twinkling stars as if listening. Or seeking a sign from the heavens. Then he leaned over the hood, his face now fully veiled in darkness.

"What if it's not a curse but a gift?"

"I use it more as a toy," I acknowledged. "Earns me some good tips at work."

"Whatever you want to call it, how about you use your superior observational skills for good instead of evil this time?"

Not sure I'd describe my efforts at big tips as *evil*, but apples and oranges.

"How?"

"To prove my wife was murdered."

My heart skittered to a stop. I knew what he was asking of me.

I knew I'd eventually say yes.

But in the immortal words of George Lucas – I had a bad feeling about this.

CHAPTER NINE

I so-o-o did not want to do it.

Two years wasn't enough time to get over betrayal by that lowdown, scum sucking excuse of a – ahem – *man*.

But if I was gonna help Bobby and find out the details from the purported suicide scene, I had to face him sooner or later. And in order to allow my feminine wiles to achieve maximum effectiveness, I'd have to do the deed in person.

No, not *that* deed. You know, mess with the guy's head. Er, uh – I mean his brains.

Oh hell, you get the picture.

Zeke Taylor. Six-foot-five, solid muscle, and Texas Ranger through-and-through. Liked his noon high and his guns and Stetson slung low.

If the Rangers still had a mounted patrol, he'd be all over that like chocolate syrup on vanilla bean ice cream.

Known as *Big Z* to his friends. And I had firsthand knowledge of how he got that nickname.

But I digress.

'Cause now we were finished. Kaput. Enemies after I caught him on a moonlit night with arms wrapped around one Lorraine Padget.

If I'd disliked her before, I wanted to field dress Lorraine's sorry carcass after that one. Like mother like daughter, I suppose. Zeke should've known better than to cross me.

'Specially with a Padget.

I was in luck, or whatever you called it when you had to face a cheating ex-boyfriend. Ranger Taylor was in residence this Monday morning, cooped up in his corner cubby of the Garland field office – or, as they preferred, Company 'B' of the Texas Ranger Division.

Honey-glazed, light brown hair peeked above the wall as I snuck up from behind. Zero pictures lined the desk. No personal effects. Not a speck of clutter save for the nondescript coffee mug.

So very Zeke.

"Hey, Stranger Ranger."

"Answer's no."

No hello. No how ya been. No checking out what he threw away. The man didn't bother turning around and continued pecking away at his computer keyboard like I wasn't even an afterthought.

I flicked my long ponytail over my shoulder and struck my best pissed-off pose.

"You can take your hand off that hip while you're at it," he continued.

"How the hell…?"

No reflection in the flat-screen monitor. Matte finish of the cubby walls weren't the source of the great reveal. No glass to project an image.

"We dated for seven months," Zeke explained. "Or have you forgotten?"

"It was eight, and yeah, I'd like to." The boy already had my dander inching toward the danger zone.

He spun the chair around to face me, tracked my image from pumps to coif, then frowned.

"I always liked your hair down better."

"Good thing I no longer care," I retorted. "It gets hot wearing it down all the time. Been thinking about cuttin' it short for the summer."

That got me a flinch.

What was it with men and long hair? Why did they make such a big deal whether we kept it long or chopped it into a pixie? Did they think the strength of our brain function was in direct correlation to the length of our hair like Samson?

I generally wore mine just above the waist, but it was still *my* hair, damnit! I say that if a man wants long hair, let him grow it himself like Jesus and the disciples and leave mine the hell alone

'Cept during those nice, slow pony rides.

Think about it.

"So where's the brochure?" Zeke asked.

It took a moment to dredge my brain up from the gutter. "Brochure?"

"Selling Girl Scout cookies or something?"

"Only in February."

"Cute."

"Even with my hair in a ponytail?" I asked.

That earned me a slow tilt of the lips. "How you doing, Vic?"

The way Zeke said my name always sounded so sultry. Like foreplay – which would never happen between us again.

I swear.

All I had to do was retrieve a certain image of the other woman to stem any naughty thoughts – no matter how the familiar whiff of his musky aftershave tried to trigger those *other* memories.

"How'd you know it was me when you were facing the other way?" I asked. "There aren't any reflective surfaces."

Zeke thumbed the phone like a hitchhiker. "They called from downstairs. Wanted to make sure you weren't on the 'no-fly' list. I told 'em to pat you down for weapons first."

"Funny. What about the hip thing?"

"Law enforcement. Unlike you, I'm paid to observe and remember things."

I crossed my arms and narrowed my eyes. "It's been two years, Sherlock. Maybe I've changed."

The eyes gave me another once over. When he finished this time, instead of a frown I got a full-blown smile. "Not a bit."

I could take that one of two ways – and I'm not sure either left me in a positive light.

"Don't even go there."

Zeke unfolded himself from the chair and rolled it my way while he leaned against the cubby counter. "Since you're not here to kiss and make up, whatcha want?"

I intended to sit in the chair as gracefully as I could. Let the power of my feminine presence work its magic. But the clearance to the floor left me dangling from the edge after my unceremonious ascent.

Didn't set the seductive tone I'd had in mind when I chose the dress this morning. Instead of the gentle hiss of lowering the ergonomic chair, it sounded more like an intermittent cow fart. If I didn't know any better, I'd think Zeke set it up high on purpose.

"If we're gonna stick with brass tacks," I said, "I'm trying to help a friend."

"This friend wouldn't happen to be named Bobby Vernet, would it?"

I bit my lip before answering. "It might."

"Not happening. Good to see you and all, but I've gotta prepare for the governor's visit."

"Now hold on a minute," I said as he almost dumped me in the floor to reacquire the chair. "You two were buds at one time. Played basketball together in high school."

"Being on the same team made us teammates, not buds." Zeke plopped into his chair, zipped it to its former heights, and started tapping away again on his keyboard. "This is a PD matter, not a Ranger one."

So that's how he wanted to play it. "Don't tell me you can't get a copy of the report."

The typing stopped.

Here's a lesson for you, ladies. The best way to get a guy's goat and get him to do what you want is to suggest he *can't* do something. Wreaks havoc on a man's ego. Remember that. Use it.

Worked every time.

The chair whipped around so fast I almost ended up in Zeke's lap. Not a totally unpleasant prospect. But considering surrounding company, not the right place or the right time.

Regardless, no matter how good the sex had been – hectic and hard or long and languid – the boy was still a lowdown, cheating son-of-a-bitch in my book.

And always would be.

"Access isn't the problem. You are."

"What's that supposed to mean?" My toe starting tapping faster than a woodpecker on a wormy piece of wood.

"You gotta stick your nose where it don't belong and come up with your own scenario to fit the scene. No matter how ridiculous."

"Well I'm not talking about Lorraine Padget here. I'm talking about Amy Vernet."

"Who committed suicide by jumping off a freakin' building. Case dismissed," Zeke said as if he were judge and jury. "And stop tapping that damned foot."

By that point, the command practically bounced off the walls of the next high-rise. My foot sped up to keep time with the boiling of my brain.

No man was ever gonna tell me what to do again. 'Specially one named Zeke Taylor. I'd pound a hole through the overpriced cheap carpet if I had to.

"First of all," I said as I shoved a finger into Zeke's face. "Why would a happily married *pregnant* woman leap to her death?"

"Appearances can be…"

"Second." My fingers followed the count. "Why'd none of her family attend the funeral?"

"Really, Vic…"

"Third. Of all the buildings in the city, why'd she jump off mine?"

That shut him up. Hallelujah and pass the offering plate to that boy. The familiar furrow of Zeke's brow suggested I'd hit upon something he hadn't considered.

I guess miracles did happen every day.

"Did you know Amy very well?" Zeke asked, curiosity getting the better of him.

"We'd had lunch together last week. All three of us, but it wasn't like we were bosom buddies or anything. Bobby said she had felt a connection to me, and for a preacher's wife she came across as rather genuine, which we both know goes a long way in my book."

Zeke rubbed a freshly shaved cheek. "Maybe she'd just found out about your previous involvement with Bobby and wanted to confront you."

"At three-thirty in the morning?"

"There's no accounting for a woman's ways…or decisions."

Not. Touching. That.

"Besides, Bobby had told her about the truck bed debacle before they even got married. And if he hadn't then, it sure would've been paramount before moving back here."

"So meeting you face-to-face set her off."

"What?"

"I can vouch for your effect on people."

That did it.

I set a glare upon him guaranteed to set Hell on fire, turned on my heel, then marched out of the office area to the elevator bank. Hell's fumes burned through my scalp while waiting for the floors to tick off until Zeke came rushing around the corner and slid to a stop before nearly slamming into me.

Graceful tall guys – aren't. Or at least only on basketball courts. Gives 'em that home court advantage.

"New shoes?" I retorted.

"Look, you bring up at least one interesting question," Zeke conceded.

"Only one? Gee, thanks."

"I'll take a hard look at the report if you'll go see Vernet and ask a little more on the family background."

"Why can't you do it?"

"Not my case," he said, blowing me off yet again. "Besides, it sounds like you already have a relationship reestablished with him."

Was that a hint of jealousy in his tone?

"Fine, I'll see what I can find out."

"Now that that's settled, I'll pick you up at six."

"What for?"

"We'll rendezvous at that little Italian place you like."

"Oh huh-uh."

"It's not a date. It's business," Zeke called over his shoulder as he walked away. "And you're buying."

"The hell I am."

"See you at six."

"My ass!"

"Maybe next time."

"Won't be a next time, Zeke Taylor!"

But he was already gone – and I had company. The older couple and the accountant type tried not to stare in the uncomfortable silence.

I sighed. The things I go through for the men in my life. Or out of my life. Or whatever.

Yeah, this was a train wreck waiting to happen – and I'd voluntarily gotten on this ride.

Yee-haw and pass me a shot of Jack.

There's just something about seeing certain exes that makes you wanna shoot something. It's far more preferable than shooting some*body*.

At least according to the law.

When that certain ex *was* the law, it was best to take said frustrations out on a thin piece of cardboard and imagine the outline with a particular face inside it.

It'd been quite some time since I'd last headed out to the range with my little Sig Sauer P938 handgun.

One reason? I'd been kinda busy.

The real reason? Zeke had bought the gun for me when we'd dated and made sure I knew how to shoot the thing on at least a weekly basis. After we broke up, I went regularly to kill that son-of-a-bitch.

Figuratively, of course.

But ammo and range fees add up right quick when you plow through rounds like a jilted lover. The gun also felt almost tainted, a constant reminder of the relationship failure. So I'd put it away on a closet shelf to gather dust.

A year or so later after a spate of muggings and rapes near the Historic West End, I figured it was best for a single gal who worked nights to have more than pepper spray for defense.

Plus, it was cute, the perfect size to fit my small hands. The rainbow purple slide also fit my personality.

Since I didn't want to lose my hearing by the time I was thirty, I usually opted for one of the outdoor ranges. What I suffered in the heat more than made up for the constant ringing from the indoor ranges – even with protection.

Of my ears, folks. Whose mind was in the gutter now?

A quick run home to change into something more appropriate and gather some gear, then I whipped the Vette toward the outskirts of the Dallas metropolis. When I arrived, the shooting was already heavy and the temps already hot.

The hefty bucket of bullets thudded at my feet as I took position in the assigned lane, checked all four magazines to make sure they had six bullets each, then snapped one in and chambered a round before sighting my target.

Let the games begin.

Most instructors will tell you to aim for center mass when seeking to take out an assailant. That's why the paper targets have the bullseye marked in the torso area.

But I always did have a thing for painting outside the lines, and figured if they didn't want me practicing headshots they wouldn't have included a head as part of the target outline.

The first shot went high somewhere off the paper. Anticipating the shot always got me in trouble, and I heard Zeke's voice in my head telling me to relax.

A roll to loosen my neck and a deep breath then I sighted again. The bullet pierced the paper near the right shoulder. Damn!

At one time I could blackout whole sections with my tight groupings. Now I couldn't even get it within the freakin' outline anymore. I really needed to get out here more often.

By the time I emptied the magazines and flicked the switch to slide the target back to my position, it was apparent I needed to get out here a hell of a lot more often.

Snickers peppered the nearby lanes before I ripped down the papier-mâché cutout that had become my target and popped in a new one.

By the time the bullet bucket was barely a fourth of the way empty, my hands and wrists were aching, and sweat ran like Niagara Falls down my back. Shoulders I'd feel tomorrow. Only an hour in and I was already done for.

A little bit longer helped me get a bit more focused before I grabbed my gear and headed for the car. A quick text exchange with Bobby and I was on track with the necessary interrogation scheduled for noon.

Gee, I was beginning to sound like an investigator already. Must be something to do with shooting off weapons instead of my disease-ridden mouth this time.

"Vic?"

The familiar voice pulled me out of the phone, but it only took a few seconds to focus in on the mustache. "Grady? What are you doing here?"

My boss set a black duffle on the ground tucked up close to his boots and shoved back his hat. "Gettin' a haircut?"

I smirked. "Yeah, okay. This is Texas. Dumb question."

The mustache tilted as he glanced from my face, down my sweaty t-shirt and shorts-clad bare legs, to the gun and magazines I'd laid atop the bullets in the bucket. "Apparently ya know what you're doin', so why haven't I ever seen ya out here before?"

"I haven't been very regular in awhile."

"You might try a laxative."

"Grady!" I laughed. "I meant coming to the gun range."

"Oh," he chuckled right along with me.

"I don't usually come out to this range though. Too many off-duty cops like to come out here."

"Like that boyfriend of yours?"

"Ex," I clarified.

The scent of manly man followed as Grady leaned in closer, his chocolate brown eyes twinkling almost golden in the sunlight.

"Good to know."

All my spit dried up in an instant as moisture headed on a more southerly trajectory. My legs went all noodley again.

Far away from my place of employment, the concept of this man being my boss whisked from my gray matter faster than a tumbleweed on the leading edge of a hurricane. Halfway expecting a kiss, I leaned closer.

Then nearly fell forward in the dust when Grady stepped backward, cradled his duffle and took off toward the range stalls.

"See ya Wednesday night," he called over his shoulder.

That's it. I really was done with men. I meant it for sure this time.

I think.

CHAPTER TEN

The Vernet clan goes through maids almost as fast as they spend Sunday morning's offering.

I wasn't sure if it was in the agreement they had with the placement service, but nine times out of ten they ended up with a bunch of Marias.

Perhaps they felt closer to God by employing someone who shared a close association to His earthly mother's given name, though I doubt if the entire crop could claim virgin status.

Either way, they didn't have to buy a bunch of new nametags every few weeks and thus saved the congregation a little bit of money.

A very little.

Personally, I suspected it was so they could put more toward Mary Jo's designer shoe collection. Or for the weekly new handbag.

Though I expect these days the savings more likely go toward Botox injections.

After a shower and third change of clothes for the day, the week's Maria escorted me into the Vernet formal living room before trudging up the winding staircase to locate Bobby.

The living room – or Blue Room as Mary Jo preferred, as if her home was the White House and she the First Lady – reflected the heights of gaudy extravagance.

Silver-gray shiny paper adorned the walls while the windows were swallowed by heavy brocade gray-blue drapes. Metallic threads were woven in so that, as Mary Jo once stated, they *captured and scattered the light as God intended.*

Matching tufted chintz sofas and chairs dotted gray carpet with far too many mirrored coffee and end tables scattered about. These were then cluttered with crystal and silver bowls, vases, and trinkets that reflected what sunlight penetrated the drapes.

The glare and inception effect threatened to bring on a headache of Biblical proportions.

After my wait extended past five minutes and the Maria-of-the-week didn't return, I decided to make myself at home and headed up the staircase. Halfway up, a door somewhere on the second floor slammed.

I stopped when another door slammed, and almost rode the banister down the staircase when Mary Jo's shrill voice echoed up the corridor.

"Don't you dare walk away from me when I'm talking to you, Robert!"

Bobby's lowered but firm voice followed. "I've left Vicki waiting long enough, Mother."

"Why did you invite her over here? That girl has already caused this family enough scandal. Don't you care how it reflects on you?"

"Don't you mean how it reflects on you and Dad?"

"Robert!"

"If you've forgotten," Bobby continued, "I'm just as much at fault for what happened. More so actually."

"If more people find out you're spending time together again, they'll assume the worst."

"That was *eleven years* ago, Mother. You're so quick to forgive me for the past, and yet you continue to hold this over her head."

"This is my house, and I don't want her in it," Mary Jo declared.

"She was in it Saturday."

"She works in a *bar*, for goodness sakes, promoting drunkenness and God knows how many other sins."

Mary Jo's sentiments didn't surprise me one bit. Matter of fact, I too was surprised she'd allowed me in her home for the funeral dinner. After my parents left, I'd half expected to be approached by some servant and escorted from the premises.

In secret, of course. Any public spectacle would've reflected poorly on Vernet and Company, and we all knew by now how they wished to avoid any spectacle where I was concerned.

Public or otherwise.

"You know," Bobby said, "I'm beginning to understand why she left the church. Seems she wasn't wanted in *that* house either."

"Robert." Mary Jo's voice ratcheted up so many octaves, she rivaled Janine for the first soprano chair. "Robert, come back here!"

A heavy gait clomped overhead. Bobby's blue eyes blazed when he saw me standing in the foyer.

"You ready?"

"Bobby, I..."

"Come on then," he said, reaching into his pants pocket and jingling his keys. "I'm driving."

"But my car's parked out front."

"Good. Maybe some of Mother's friends will stop by and see it and assume the worst." A wicked grin adorned Bobby's face.

There's the guy I knew and loved. Liked. Was friends with.

Oh, forget it.

Bobby drove his BMW X-5 as if he was back on a third world mission field. He plowed through the suburbs of Dallas, hanging onto the steering wheel like a python clinging to and praying over its last meal.

Or maybe that was me.

"So," I started, clutching the door arm in a death grip. "How's your mom?"

Didn't even get me a glance. "You heard her."

"All of Dallas heard her."

A Texas-sized grunt was the only response.

"Do you think she'll have my car towed?"

"And draw more attention to the fact it's in front of their house?" he growled. "I doubt it."

"Gee, that makes me feel so much better."

Bobby made a lane change and slowed as the exit drew near. "I'm really sorry you had to hear all that. I'll never understand her unforgiving attitude toward you."

I patted his knee. "You're her little lamb chop. 'Course she'll forgive you."

"I'm almost thirty," he grumbled.

"Age doesn't stop the parental patrol."

"The way she's acting, you'd think I hadn't lived a day on my own over the last decade. That I'd never been married."

The mention of marriage shut him up real fast. Red rimmed his eyes and the bob of his Adam's apple reflected the dogged fight against tears. I left him in tortured peace until we pulled up to the restaurant in the heart of the Historic West End.

My usual haunts. "This is an odd area for a pastor to patronize. Are you sure it's safe for you to be seen around here?"

"Even Jesus consorted with sinners, Vicki."

"Like me?"

Bobby hung his head and sighed. "I just want to have a chance to talk without interruption. Without judgment."

"Amen to that, brother."

That earned me the quirk of a smile as we strolled across the parking lot. I was recognized the instant we entered the murky grill and bar.

"A little early in the day for you around here, ain't it?" the old proprietor called.

"Having lunch with a friend," I responded.

Thick gray eyebrows lifted before a toothy grin spread across the loveable buzzard's face. "What'll it be then?"

"Whatever's on tap for me and a coke for him," I said with a thumb in Bobby's direction.

After settling in a dim corner booth away from windows, and any accompanying prying eyes, we ordered a couple of burgers and nursed our drinks.

Bobby stirred the ice around and stared into his pop as if in a trance. After all the years apart, I hated seeing him in such a funk.

Time to call this meeting to order. "I went to see Zeke this morning."

Blue eyes rose from the swirling syrup in surprise. "Zeke Taylor?"

"That's the one," I acknowledged.

"I thought he'd moved to Austin." Bobby tilted his head in thought. "Wanted to become a Ranger, didn't he?"

"He did, and he did. Transferred to Company 'B' a few years ago to help his dad with the ranch after the accident. We went out a couple of times a few months ago, so I thought he might be a good place to start."

I know what you're thinking. *Couple* of dates? *Few* months ago?

Hell, who cared about semantics at a time like this. No need to stir up any bad blood between those two where I was concerned.

Long story.

"And?" Bobby urged.

"He asked me to go on a fishing expedition with you."

"Let me guess. He thinks Amy and I were putting on a good show for the public."

"Nailed it."

The moment the plates slid across the table, Bobby laid into the burger as if he'd forgotten to eat for days. Considering the turmoil over Amy's death, that was a distinct possibility. After a couple of enormous bites and replenishment of our drinks, he slowed enough to voice some mental musings.

"Can't blame Zeke for thinking that about me. I got pretty good at pretending for public consumption in my younger years."

"We learned from some of the best," I said, clinking my beer against his glass and nearly sloshing both into his lap.

Graceful I'm not – in far too many ways these days.

When Bobby took another drink and grimaced, I suspected a little beer had clashed with his coke.

"The thing is, Amy and I were happier than I'd ever imagined possible after what I'd witnessed with my parents. We cleared the air early on in our relationship and that offered openness and trust in our marriage. We talked about everything. Shared everything. I was free to be completely myself. Accepted for who I was."

The awe and rawness in his admission choked me up almost as much as it did him.

Talk about crying in your beer.

But like the consummate professional I'd become when it came to emotions, I held those pesky tears at bay and offered up what I hoped was a sympathetic look. Knowing my luck, it probably looked more like I tried to clench a fart.

Then another unexpected emotion almost bitch-slapped me before I was even aware of it. The little green monster of envy jumped on my spine and held on like a cowboy riding a bronco.

Could I ever be so open with someone like that? Could I ever let someone know me so completely? How could I when I didn't even know myself?

For a moment, I longed for what Bobby had discovered with Amy.

Danger! Danger! Approaching enemy territory. I wasn't ready to delve too deep into my own psyche.

At least not yet.

I tackled Bobby's claim instead. "I posed a couple of questions to Zeke that intrigued him enough to look into the case."

"Really?"

Bobby's tear-filled eyes held so much hope and faith in me, I almost stopped myself right then from pursuing things any further. But if I was gonna continue to ride this wagon train, I had to broach the questions I'd posed to Zeke.

The first was obviously off the table after Bobby's description of marital bliss, so I started in with question two. "Why was none of Amy's family at the funeral?"

Bobby pushed fries around his plate, chose one then swirled it in a mound of ketchup. "Amy's mom died from a drug overdose a couple of years ago. It's what brought us back from serving in Central America."

That unexpected admission stopped me. For a sec. "Drugs?"

"Yeah." Bobby nodded. "Her mom was a lifelong user, though she was high functioning even after so many years. I'd never have known it at our wedding if Amy hadn't warned me beforehand."

Drug use – that brought on a whole slew of possibilities for what happened to Amy.

But it still didn't explain the rest of her family's absence at the funeral. "What about her dad?"

"Amy never knew her father."

Talk about your church ladies gone wild. If the tongue waggers at the church got ahold of that juicy morsel, they'd be busy for months gnawing on that bone.

As open as Amy was, I doubt she would've shared this tainted tidbit anytime soon. Even with me, regardless of the cosmic connection she'd felt between us.

"Did your mom and dad know Amy's secrets?" I asked.

"See, that's the thing," Bobby returned. "Amy never thought of them as secrets. They were simply a part of her life's journey. Challenges that steered her toward a better life, though she'd have done anything to rescue her mom from drugs. And she tried." Bobby's face clouded with anger. "But my parents were insistent Amy keep her *dirty laundry* out of the church."

"*Her* dirty laundry? Not like it was Amy's fault her mom chose to get mixed up in drugs or sleep around."

Pot, meet kettle.

"Didn't stop my mom from thinking of her as the devil's spawn though."

The burger slid sideways down my throat. I coughed so hard the stuck steer splashed right into my beer.

"Did she really call Amy that?" I asked as I fished around in my drink.

"Might as well have. The phrase *Mexican trash* spewed out of her mouth only an hour ago."

"But Amy was your wife," I replied in horror.

Bobby shrugged and sighed, dropping the ketchup-drenched fry as if he'd lost his appetite. "Nothing's changed in the years since I left. Seems all Mother cares about is appearances. And Amy didn't measure up in her mind."

"When it comes to your mom, no woman ever could."

A fact I knew that firsthand.

I wanted to march right over to the Vernet mansion and hose down Mary Jo with warm beer. Host a cow chip throwing contest on their front lawn.

No, wet t-shirt night. That'd get the neighbors talking. But we'd never get everyone past security.

Hell, *I* probably would never get past security again after today. I only hoped my day pass didn't expire before retrieving my car.

Bobby cradled his head in his hands. "Now do you understand why I had to get away all those years ago?"

"I'm getting an inkling."

"My parents make it almost impossible to practice the command to honor thy father and mother whenever I'm anywhere within a five-hundred mile radius. For any chance to find a real relationship with the Lord, a real relationship with any woman, I had to escape the family trappings."

He pushed his plate aside and looked me square in the eyes straight from his tormented soul. "Am I making any sense, Vicki?"

More than you know, Bobby Boy. More than you know.

CHAPTER ELEVEN

Does sharing two different meals with two different guys in one day make me a certified slut?

Don't answer that.

After a lifetime of dining in some of the most expensive and glamorous five-star restaurants around the world, I'd come to discover that expensive didn't necessarily mean tasty. Most of the time it translated into exotic, strange, and just downright unappetizing.

At least to this youngster.

I mean, what kid wants to roll a dollop of slimy snail around in her mouth, regardless of the wasted fifty bucks?

Ugh!

But when the status of my pocketbook changed after my flight to freedom, Zeke had introduced me to some of the best food Dallas had to offer. What the dives lacked in ambience and aesthetics they more than made up for in mouthwatering deliciousness.

At reasonable prices to boot.

Even so, my favorite Italian dive *La Buona Cibo Vino* tipped the top of my wallet's current scale.

Financial concerns melted away with my first bite of shrimp manicotti. "Mmm. It's been too long."

Zeke cocked an eyebrow. "Stopped coming to our place after you stormed away?"

I wouldn't dignify Zeke's attempt to goad me. "More like out of financial considerations."

"Things that bad?" Though his apparent concern didn't stop him from shoveling it in.

"Just restocking the coffers."

"Because?"

"Not that it's any of your business, but the Vette needed some heavy-duty maintenance this year and set me back a pretty penny."

That got me a snort. "That car is a money pit. Don't know why you keep it."

"Because it's *my* money pit," I said. "A gift that keeps on giving." Or taking in this case.

"But I know how you feel about the giver."

Namely one Frankie Bohanan. "Well it's my name on the title, and that's all that matters." I plopped another bite of manicotti in my mouth for good measure and smiled around the cheese.

After all the cotillion training, Mom would be ashamed if she saw me, though she should've realized I was a lost cause after I threw up all over the floor on my first day of kindergarten.

Or after tripping over the threshold entering a swanky restaurant after church on Sunday and exposing my Hello Kitty undies to an astonished crowd.

Then there was the time I tore down the aisle of the old church during the kid's Christmas production, ruining my grand entrance as the Virgin Mary and launching the Baby

Jesus doll into the audience to escape the rampaging donkey colt.

Zeke just shook his head as if he'd had a front row seat to my walk down memory lane. "So why're you really snooping around for Bobby? Hoping to jump back on that bandwagon now that the wife is out of the way?"

I so wanted to spit cheese in Zeke's face. "That's a horrible thing to say, Zeke Taylor. What would your mother think?"

"Why don't we call her and ask?" A wicked grin split his face as Zeke reached for his phone.

"And give that poor woman more to worry about when you don't get home safe tonight?" I threatened.

"Depends on where I end up." Heat warmed those brown eyes as long, agile and very capable fingers inched closer to his cell.

"Try the morgue."

He picked up his fork instead. "I'm just saying, there are some factions who might connect the dots between the present circumstances and the past you two shared."

"You saying you're one of those factions?"

"Well now, you always were good at playing us against each other in high school."

"You're thinking of Lorraine Padget."

That stopped him for a sec. "Nah, I was thinking of you and me."

"There is no you and me. There is no me and him. Bobby was my friend. *Is* my friend," I clarified. "And he always will be. Nothing more. That's it. Case closed."

"You wish," Zeke mumbled into his loaded meat-lovers lasagna.

I ignored the jab, but it got me thinking. Was my past with Bobby really a closed deal?

Sure he was finger-lickin' good-looking. Yeah my heart did a little pitty-pat where Bobby was concerned. And my panties still rode the tilt-a-whirl on occasion.

But the guy was a pastor now, which was a no-go in my book. There's no way I'd ever desire to hold the title of *pastor's wife*, so why bother admiring the goods on the shelf?

Besides, the shelf life on my virginity expired a long time ago, and we all knew by now what Mary Jo Vernet thought of that. This here outlaw putting up with the Vernets as in-laws?

A big nuh to the uh.

Bobby and me a couple?

Not even an option.

"If you're done living in the past, let's bring this meeting to order in the present," I urged in my best Judge Judy voice, tapping my fork on the table like a gavel.

"Fine. Did you talk to Bobby then?"

"I did."

"And?"

"He and Amy had a very open marriage."

Interest sparked his attention. "Open as in..."

"Honesty, Zeke. Open and honest," I said. "Gee, get your mind out of the gutter."

"Sounds to me like yours is the mind that's gutter bound."

"Hey, if you want me to pick up tonight's tab, you better lay off."

"What about the lack of family at Amy's funeral?" Zeke asked, zeroing in and right back on track like a good Ranger.

"Bobby said her mom died of a drug overdose a couple of years ago," I offered. "I understand she was a lifelong user."

"Father?"

"Never knew him."

While Zeke chewed on that thought, I signaled a wine refill from the waiter. If my checkbook balance was gonna drop tonight, it might as well go down happy.

Or at least make me feel happy so I could wake up feeling like I got something out of the night. After all, Zeke drove so I could drink all I wanted.

Then again, wine always did things to me. Strange things. Made me feel all warm and gooey inside. Warm enough to do something really stupid if I wasn't careful.

One more glass wouldn't hurt, but then I'd have to call it quits. I already had Nick complicating my life. The boss too. Now Bobby, but in a different way. Cross my heart.

No matter how many nights I'd laid awake counting F-150s.

Oh man. Maybe I was a slut riding the express train straight to Hell.

I dropped my fork into the manicotti and sighed.

"What's eatin' you?" Zeke asked.

I glared. "Really poor choice of words right about now."

That got me a smirk and an intense – and interested – stare from molten eyes edging toward ebony. Sent my womb into a swoon.

I clenched my thighs together with a firm mental *no* and reminded my wine-soaked brain of Zeke's two-timing ways with the pageanted Padget. Then there was that resolve to stave off men.

Yeah, yeah, I know. It hadn't worked with Nick either. Don't remind me.

Zeke continued with the questions. "Did Bobby have any idea why Amy was at your building then?"

I shook my head. "Last thing he remembered was hearing her get up that night, assuming she was going to the bathroom. Pregnancy and all that, you know."

"I wouldn't know," Zeke replied.

Good to know. "*Anyway*, he must've gone right back to sleep since he didn't hear the car start."

"Where's their bedroom in proximity to the garage?"

"Haven't a clue. Never been to their house."

Zeke cocked a brow in disbelief.

What was it with all the suspicion? I usually got it from the church crowd, but I don't think Zeke has sat in the family pew for a few years. Longer than me even.

"Garage doors cause quite a racket," he mused aloud.

"They just moved in though. Maybe the car wasn't in the garage."

"How 'bout you do me a favor then? Surprise Bobby with a visit to get the lay of the land."

"That might work." I took a big bite of lukewarm shrimp manicotti, and quickly located my napkin. "What about your end? Did you check the case file? See any good reason to poke your nose in it?"

Zeke pushed his empty plate away before tipping back the remainder of wine like throwing down a shot. His tongue curled to capture a drop at the edge of his lip. My pulse skipped its usual rhythm as I recalled the talents in that tongue.

And I ain't talking syntax.

Had someone turned the air conditioning off in here? I gulped ice water to temper my enflamed memories. Yeah, I'd definitely had too much wine.

"The report is pretty straight-forward," Zeke stated. "No appearance of struggle on the rooftop. None of your neighbors reported hearing anything out of the ordinary. By all appearances, the scene suggests suicide."

"What about toxicology?"

Zeke leaned forward and touched my fingertips. "You were always good at talking my language."

The right thing to do in that moment would've been to remove my hand, but the familiar zing of his touch sent luxuriating chills down my spine to my overactive nether regions. My brain turned sluggish as I stared at my empty glass. How much wine had I drunk?

"And?" It was the only answer I could get past my thick tongue.

"An over-the-counter sedative was discovered in her system."

"Wouldn't that be dangerous to take while pregnant?"

"I called the M.E. It's commonly used, even during pregnancy."

I finally succeeded in convincing my brain to remove my hands from the table to my lap. "So you share the police department's conclusion?"

"I didn't say that."

"So what are you saying, Ranger Taylor?"

"Something's missing from the report."

My turn to lean forward in breathless anticipation, and it wasn't because of Zeke's musky scent.

I swear.

"What's missing?"

His nose hovered mere inches from mine, and I felt the brush of his breath on my lips when he spoke.

"Footprints."

CHAPTER TWELVE

Cars in the driveway? Check.

The question of vehicle location crossed off my list as I rounded the corner onto Bobby's tree-lined street and saw the moving boxes crammed into the open garage. A few were piled along the sidewalk for the sanitation crew, and Bobby added one more as I parked along the curb with a wave – and received a half-hearted one in return.

Hmm. Rough day.

My day wasn't shaping up much better. Mom had acted none too thrilled when I'd cut our Tuesday luncheon short and skipped out on afternoon shopping. You would've thought she'd be happy with the credit card reprieve, but it didn't stop the barrage of questions she peppered my way.

Where're you going?
Who will you be with?
Who will you really be with?
Why can't you go another day?
This doesn't have anything to do with Robert, does it?

'Course I expertly deflected all of the questions. For the most part.

Maybe.

If Mom smelled any hint of my true destination, she would've bashed me over the head and tossed my carcass in her trunk faster than I could down a shot of Jack. Actually, she'd probably have had a waiter do it to avoid messing up her manicure.

But I digress.

Bobby squinted through the sunlight and scowled at my gauzy, white dress. "Don't tell me you're gonna help in that?"

I pulled a bag from the passenger's seat and slung the strap over my sore shoulders. Yesterday's target practice had already come back to haunt me. Helping Bobby move boxes today was gonna be the final thing to send my muscles packing.

Or, in this case, unpacking.

"Brought a change of clothes," I called.

"Well, come on then."

His jeans and t-shirt were coated with dust and marred with sweat.

Tell me, ladies, why is it that guys still look good even when they're grimy? Bobby and Zeke had always been sweaty and stinky after winning a high school basketball game – and I still would've given my right arm to have had them lay a big one on me.

But girls? We women were expected to look picture perfect at all times. Our hair in place, makeup perfect, and clothes neat even after playing a round of coed softball in the middle of July. Or after hitting the shooting range.

Life wasn't fair.

An older lady perched on the porch next door. I could only imagine what she thought as I traipsed up the walk into the house with my duffle in tow.

I could see the headline – *Pastor Who Just Lost Wife and Unborn Child Brings in Another Woman Before the Bodies are Cold*.

Some people would probably go so far as to misconstrue I carried an overnight bag. I so wanted to run over and explain to the sweet old lady it wasn't what it appeared, even though I'd used this sucker before as an overnight bag. But I had no intention to this time around.

I swear.

Bobby didn't seem too concerned as he directed me into the modest three or four-bedroom home, up the stairs, and to a spare room with an assortment of sturdy and wilted boxes in varying stages of unpacking. The pile of royal blue Christian Bible Fellowship High School t-shirts brought back some interesting memories.

"Nice shirts."

"Yeah." Bobby stared absently at the pile. "I was planning to do something special for my alma mater while the baseball team finished their season, but it's kinda taken a backseat."

"Understandable."

"You can leave your stuff on the bed there." Bobby waved in the general direction before his eyes shifted and an unusual hardness settled in them. "I've given up on this room for now."

"I'll join you in a flash."

As I got dressed, I considered my cute little shorts to his practical jeans. I tugged on the lacy tank and stared in the mirror at the cleavage while I wrapped my hair in a loopy pigtail. The nosy neighbor had me reconsidering my choice of apparel.

That thought got my dander up.

There was nothing going on between me and Bobby. I had no intentions toward him anymore, regardless of what others might think of my clothes.

So then why did we have to justify any and all association?

Already I'd had to tiptoe around my mom. And now the nosy nana next door. I was here to assist a friend. Period. End of story.

Well, and get some information like I'd promised Zeke. But that was it.

After borrowing a blue t-shirt from the stack to better conceal what God gave me, I marched into the hall and glanced through each doorway.

Question number two – check. The master bedroom was upstairs and toward the rear of the house while the driveway and road were toward the front on the opposite end.

The cars positioned along the drive instead of in the cram-packed garage made it clear Amy could easily have left the house in the middle of the night without disturbing Bobby. Most guys slept so hard a nearby bomb blast might not awaken them. A girl could sneak in or out without waking anyone when she needed.

At least that was my experience. Experiences.

Bobby had been busy in the garage while I'd explored. A neat path carved its way between the stacks toward the open garage door, where he kicked a box and sent it sailing into the grass like a field goal attempt.

'Cept there weren't any hash marks or uprights in the yard to gauge the distance.

"Score," I yelled, throwing my arms up like a referee in the end zone and immediately regretted the movement as my muscles protested.

That only got me a glare and a huff. So much for trying to lighten the mood.

"Oka-a-ay." I tied the shirttail in a knot at my hip. "Anything I should know about?"

"Nothing much," Bobby snarked. "Just that Amy's mom was a cotton-pickin' liar."

"I thought she was…um…gone?"

Remember that avoidance thing? It's my specialty, folks.

In this instance, I dodged using the words *dead, deceased,* or the usually appropriate phrase *passed on,* 'cause they wouldn't do anything for Bobby's current state. The substituted football in the yard maintained his stare like he'd light the thing on fire with the power of his mind.

Or perhaps he prayed God would smite it.

"She is," he muttered. "But that doesn't stop her from continuing to screw with our lives."

"Issues with the in-laws," I said with a nod. "Common problem with marriages, or so I've heard."

"You don't know the half of it." Shoulders slumped and the fight appeared to drain right out of him before Bobby turned to the never-ending boxes and settled on the wilted ones at the front. "Help me drag these to the curb, will you?"

They looked like the ones from the spare bedroom I'd changed in upstairs. "Aren't you gonna go through them first?"

"I don't want to know anymore of her secrets."

"Whoa. I didn't think Amy kept secrets from you."

"Not Amy." Bitterness seethed between Bobby's teeth. "Her mother."

A couple of lawn chairs were smushed into the far corner. I rescued them and set them up in the shade at the edge of the garage to catch a furnace-like breeze and where Nosy Nana couldn't see us. Since my arms felt like I'd already spent hours maneuvering boxes, I had no qualms about putting off additional strain a bit longer.

I plopped down in a chair and patted the other. "You look like you could use a break there, pardner. Take a load off for a sec and do a little 'splaining to this confused cowgirl before you do something rash like kick the neighbor's dog."

"Gee, thanks."

Bobby snatched a couple of water bottles from an ice chest, handed me one and took a swig from the other, before sitting down with a sigh. Sweat from the humid afternoon trickled down his temples, and he smelled like he'd just played a round of one-on-one with the guys.

Ah, the memories. "Tell me what's got you all worked up today."

"I don't feel much like talking," he returned.

Leave it to a man to clam up when he should be getting things off his chest. "Then you can listen."

Even though I hadn't done any heavy lifting yet, I was still hotter than a woman in the throes of menopause and tucked the water bottle down the shirt neck to rest between my boobs.

Living in Texas all my life hadn't acclimated me to the heat and humidity of a good ol' southern summertime. That was one reason I covered as little as I could legally get away with.

Personally, I'd rather live somewhere north. Like the Arctic Circle.

I dove in. "Found out something interesting from Zeke last night."

Bobby glanced at the moisture outlining the water bottle under my shirt. "You two have a hot date?"

I tossed him my best ticked-off look. "Just business."

"Not what I heard."

"Since when did you join the gossiping gaggle?"

"I imagine the information was an attempt by my mother to discourage my spending time with you." He air quoted around the bottle in his hand. "Now that I'm *single* again."

"Well, tell your mother that you were the one who asked for my help."

"I did."

"And Zeke is the only law enforcement officer I know well enough to ask a favor."

"I figured."

"We're just friends, you know."

"Uh-huh." Bobby took a long gulp of water.

Zeke a friend? Not sure I'd go so far as to consider us that. We hadn't spoken to each other in the more than two years since the epic breakup – or breakdown, depending on how you saw it.

Sharing a meal last night had been nice at times. That is until Zeke opened his mouth and reminded me how good he was at frustrating the life out of me.

But he truly was the only LEO I knew well enough to ask about the police report. That didn't mean I hadn't *known* a few others.

You know – in the Biblical sense.

"Why don't you just get Zeke to help you instead of using me as the middleman?" I asked. "Save us all a heap of headaches."

He tossed the half-full water bottle up in the air a few times as if stalling. "Zeke and I had a bit of a falling out in high school."

"Please tell me it wasn't over Lorraine Padget."

"Besides," Bobby said, completely ignoring my comment. "I know how good you are at sizing people up at first glance. Amy was a lot like you in that regard…gifted with discernment."

At one time, I too thought I was good at sizing people up. Had a lot of fun with it at the bar these days, though it didn't always seem like a gift.

Zeke's betrayal had cured me of that delusion.

"Speaking of Amy, do you want to know what Zeke found in the report? Or should I say *didn't* find?"

"You've got my attention."

"So my apartment building is old, right?" I started in.

"Um, okay," Bobby responded.

"It's got one of those flat asphalt roofs with a rubber liner sealing it."

"Yeah?"

"So why didn't she leave any foot imprints leading from the door to…"

"…the edge," Bobby finished as realization dawned across his face.

"There should've been pictures of shoe prints in the file, references of dimensions and stuff in the write-up. At least that's what Zeke said."

Bobby swiped a hand across his eyes as if wiping away sweat, but the shallow cough gave him away. Pain and heartache radiated from him.

I hesitated. We'd already gone this far, and the next question begged to be asked.

I approached it gently. "This leads into another question."

A deep breath rattled as his head drooped. "Shoot."

"Did Amy ever use any over-the-counter sleep aids?"

Bobby's brow furrowed as he raised his head. "Not that I ever knew."

My earlier glance into the master bedroom hadn't revealed anything on the nightstands but a couple of Bibles, books and a notepad. Discretion had kept me from rifling through drawers and the medicine cabinet, so I had to take his word for it.

Hey, it was Bobby's bedroom. I had no intention of crossing that threshold ever again – real or imagined.

"We have a bonafide mystery on our hands then," I said.

"How so?"

"It just so happens a heap of the stuff was found in her system."

CHAPTER THIRTEEN

In the two-and-a-half years in my apartment, I'd had few reasons to bother the super. Paid my rent on time and took extra special care of my place.

Mostly.

Plus, when the bi-annual pest control notice hit my door, I made certain me and my cuddly critter became scarce.

'Cause Jimmy's appearance kinda gave me the creeps, what with the scars across his cheek and forehead like a gang war survivor. One side of his mouth even drooped like the nerves had been cut deep under the surface, drool dripping like a ravenous wolf baring its fangs.

Maybe that was more an active imagination on my part. Or too many horror movies.

Yeah, we'll chalk it up to that.

It had always surprised me though that he'd been entrusted with such a job. You know, being the *face* of the building and all.

Even though Jimmy had always been nice to me – or more like indifferent – on the rare occasion we interacted, I never felt altogether comfortable in his presence.

So after cleaning up from assisting Bobby all afternoon, I trudged my squeaky-clean carcass down three flights of stairs to stand before apartment one-oh-two.

I stood.

And stood.

Working up some cowardly lion courage, I finally rapped on the door – and froze when Jimmy's massive bulk filled the doorway.

Three hundred pounds, give or take, and solid muscle through and through stared me down. His bicep was bigger than my waistline and the skull tattoo winked at me when he flexed.

We grow our boys big in the Texas sun. The brawn comes from God. The scary part?

I didn't wanna know.

"Vicki, right?" Jimmy asked.

"Uh, right. From, um, four-oh-seven," I stuttered in shock.

The guy had a good memory, considering the number of tenants in the building. Couple that with the fact I didn't regularly bother him, and color me impressed with his cognitive function.

Or creeped out even more 'cause he knew who I was. I wasn't *that* memorable.

Was I?

"Havin' a problem?" Jimmy prompted.

"Not exactly a problem per se. More like a question."

"Bout what? And make it quick," he said as he glanced behind the door.

He might be entertaining company, though I had a hard time thinking any woman wouldn't run away screaming when confronted by his sheer size, much less due to all the tats and scars. There was no accounting for some women's taste in men.

Hear that Lorraine Padget?

"It's about that woman who committed suicide last week."

Dark eyes trailed me up then down as if truly noticing me for the first time. When they rested again on my face, the window to the soul snapped shut so fast I almost heard the *thunk*.

"You some sort of PI now?" he asked.

"Nope," I assured. "Just a bartender."

"Why're ya asking questions about that woman then?"

"Got a...friend. With the Rangers." Eyes narrowed before I sputtered out the rest. "But we don't talk much anymore."

"So if y'all don't talk anymore, why's he still a friend?"

"Wait a minute," I said. "Why do you assume he's a he and not a she?"

"Cause he used to be around often enough."

The creep factor went up about ten degrees. Or twenty.

"H-how would you know?"

"It's my job to observe what's going on in my building."

First Zeke. Now Jimmy. Is it a requirement of manhood to be observant?

While girls are in cotillion training, do they offer classes to guys like *Habits of Highly Effective Observers*?

Perhaps something like *How to Spot an Available Female*.

Or there's my favorite one of *How to Tell When a Guy is Hitting on Your Girl*.

Now there's a class I could teach in the reverse. I mean, I was pretty observant, but mainly I checked out clothes, hair, and hygiene, not to mention the ring finger on the left hand – and making sure there was no hint of a tan line.

Maybe I should've been a guy.

"So does that mean you saw something that night?" I ventured.

Jimmy hesitated and glanced again behind the door. "Wrap this up or come in for a spell. I gotta steak on the grill."

Enter the lion's den? Willingly? Heaven help me. My knocking knees must have made a cacophonous clattering noise.

Jimmy rolled his eyes. "Can you at least wait here so I can flip it before it's beyond saving?"

All I could get out as I stared at Jimmy's scars was, "Uh-huh."

The door remained propped open as Jimmy lumbered across his living room. The rumble of sliding glass doors followed, and I caught a whiff of sizzling beef. My mouth watered and stomach betrayed me when I realized it was well into the dinner hour.

One of the benefits to living on the ground floor was residents had a fenced-in, postage stamp sized patch of lawn on which pooches could piddle. Personally, I rather liked the additional security of living upwardly mobile.

But having a balcony with an outdoor grill would sure make a nice addition. Maybe the landlord would take that into consideration when it came time to renovate.

Then again, if my eighties-style kitchen was any indicator, renovations weren't on the agenda anytime soon.

Jimmy returned, dabbing saliva from the drooping edge of his mouth. Something in his expression had changed. Softened.

"So what'd ya wanna know?" he asked with a sigh.

"I'm kinda a friend of the family," I said.

"Was the woman here for you that night then?"

"That's what has me stumped. I worked until late that night and didn't get home until around three-thirty."

"You do keep interesting hours."

You know that eerie tingle up your spine just before the killer in the movies jumps out from the darkness and slashes a character across the throat? Yeah, me too. Feeling it right now as a matter of fact.

Not pleasant.

"Anyway," I continued, squelching my movie-induced imagination. "Some of the family isn't convinced it was a suicide."

Jimmy looked me up and down then sneered. "Do they think *you* dragged her up and tossed her off?"

"No. Can I ask the questions please?"

The bicep skull winked again as Jimmy glanced over his shoulder. "My steak's 'bout done so make it quick."

"How would she have gotten to the roof in the first place?" I quickly asked.

"The stairwell."

"But I understand the roof access is always locked 'cept for maintenance."

Something connected in Jimmy's brain as a light dawned from behind his guarded gaze. "That's somethin' I didn't stop to think about the other night."

Stupidity prodded my next question. "Don't you have the key?"

"Yeah."

"Anyone else?"

"Just me and the landlord, far as I know," Jimmy said before anger-tinged fire flashed in his eyes. "Wait a sec. What're ya saying?"

"Nothing, I…"

"You got somethin' to accuse me of?" The beefy body filled the doorframe as Jimmy stepped across the threshold into the hall, his voice deepening to a thunderous roar. "Think I've been negligent and left the door unlocked? That *I* killed that woman?"

"No, no, I just…"

The fires of Hell scented the hallway as I backed away. Smoke rose steadily from Jimmy's collar and spewed from his nostrils.

No wait – it was in the background. Coming from his living room.

Jimmy swung around to face his doorway. "Damnit, woman. Now you've gone and made me burn my dinner."

As I scooted and stumbled my way up the staircase, the slam of Jimmy's apartment door rattled like Dallas was having an earthquake. I was not looking forward to the next extermination visit.

Maybe it was time to reconsider my living arrangements. Bring in a roommate for protection.

I could see the ad now: *Notice – roommate wanted. Must be willing to tolerate a steady stream of cute guys, a cuddly cat, and quarters with questionable characters.*

They don't call me Scaredy Cat Bohanan for nothing.

CHAPTER FOURTEEN

You know how you feel in the mornings after using muscles you forgot you had? Yeah, me too.

'Cept this time it was from lifting and dragging boxes across Bobby's yard and into the house after I was already sore from shooting. I ached like a runner training for a marathon. Like a weightlifter for a competition. Like a…

Oh, hell. Morning had arrived entirely too early and without my brain in tow.

The insistent buzz of my cell phone demanded attention even though everything in me screamed to throw it at the wall. But that'd leave me without communication to the outside world.

Hmm. Tempting as the thought was at the moment, I really couldn't spend money on unnecessary expenses right now.

After prying my eyelids apart to stare at a too-bright screen illuminating my dark bedroom, I counted three missed calls from Janine.

Wait – why was the phone lighting up my room?

Why was my apartment still so dark?

Five o'clock? As in A.M.? What the…?

"What the hell, Janine?" I yelled into my phone.

The buzzing continued. It echoed throughout my apartment and seeped through the open bedroom door from the living room.

I flopped out of bed with a groan and sprawled across the carpet as my foot tangled in the sheets. Slinky slid off alongside me then scuttled under the bed with a scowl and accompanying yowl.

I was gonna kill her.

Or maybe Nick was at the door looking for a morning booty call. Couldn't the guy go a couple of days without release? I knew I could. Sometimes. Not always.

Warmth flushed my skin at the thought. Someone was about to get the full brunt of some sleep-deprived, muscle tormented, sexually frustrated female in her skivvies.

Come what may.

I ripped open the front door, which closed just as quickly when the attached security chain rebounded. In my frustrated and fumbling state, it took a moment to disengage the stupid and utterly worthless thing before opening the door again.

"What the hell, Janine?" I attempted again as my best friend's disheveled mug filled my doorway.

"Bobby's been arrested!"

Have you ever had one of those moments where a single sentence both wakes *and* shuts you up faster than a tornado rips your roof off?

I plead the fifth.

Most Rangers live pretty close to their respective offices in order to get there at a moment's notice. At least that's what Zeke led me to believe when we were dating.

It finally had the chance to see the logic behind it. Even at just after five in the A.M., driving from near Dallas's West End to Garland left me snarled in traffic. What was at most a twenty-minute trip under normal circumstances doubled, tripled, and quadrupled with the early morning rush hour.

Then again there was little that could be classified as *normal* when it came to Dallas traffic. Rush hour? What a joke. On both fronts. There was little *rush* and definitely more than an *hour* to get anywhere when it came right down to it.

As my Vette inched along toward the I-635 interchange, I snatched up my phone and tried Zeke again. Yes, even though we'd been split up for years, his number was still firmly implanted in my cell phone database. Emergencies only.

Bite me.

A growl filled my ear. "Unless you're on the way over, I suggest you hang up before someone gets hurt."

I snorted. "I'm on the way over, but not for what you want, you idiot."

"The idiot is hanging up now."

"Don't you dare, Zeke Taylor. Not after I dragged my butt out at this ungodly hour." I laid on my horn to dissuade the fender encroacher beside me trying to sneak into my lane.

"Wait, did you say you're on your way over?" Zeke asked with a little more clarity in his question.

"Are you awake now?"

"Yeah, but why are you?"

"Cause Janine showed up at my apartment to inform me Bobby's been arrested," I said. "And she went back home to get ready for her classes only after I promised to immediately find out why."

Two beats later. "Let me make some calls. What's your ETA?"

"Whenever I can weed through this God-forsaken traffic."

"I'll have answers and coffee when you get here," Zeke offered. "Bring donuts."

"I'm not your personal waitress."

"Make sure one's an apple fritter."

"Asshole," I muttered as he hung up. I tossed the phone into the console.

I'm not a morning person. Never been a morning person. You want me bleary-eyed and bitchy? Wake me any time before ten and that's all you were gonna get. Zeke was in for a real treat alright.

And its name wasn't *apple fritter*.

After muscling my way through traffic then swinging through a donut drive-thru for an apple fritter, bear claw, and a couple of chocolate iced, I made it to Zeke's Country Hoedown by six twenty-five.

Pink and orange tinged the sky as I made my way past the security gate and parked. The high-rise building offered the latest innovations of modern living space, though I doubted if Zeke had ever used anything in the kitchen.

'Cept the coffeemaker, of course.

You could take the boy away from the ranch, but that didn't mean he left it all behind. I'd bet a hundred dollars he still had the longhorn steer head on the wall for hanging his hats on the horns. And that nasty deerskin rug in the living room – ugh.

What about that tree ring coffee table resting on the antler stool? Bet he'd gone and killed Bambi's mother just to get 'em.

'Course I completely missed all that when Zeke greeted me at his door with nothing but a towel hanging low on his hips. Chiseled abs and cut pecs begged me to run my fingers through the dark mass of chest curls.

Did the air just spike a thousand degrees?

Yeah, that's what I thought.

Ignoring my hot and bothered state, Zeke grabbed the donut box, shoved the apple fritter into his mouth, then headed toward the kitchen with a mumble of what I could only assume was some sort of hello.

I shut the front door and let my nose lead me by the scent of fresh-brewed coffee. A full cup with milk added and, what I hoped was two sugars, sat waiting on the modern cement countertop. I didn't even have to ask if it was mine.

Now Zeke? He drank it straight. Black like any good cowboy. Or as God intended. Or whatever other reason he'd come up with for the day.

When he gravitated toward one of my chocolates after inhaling the fritter, I slapped his hand away. "Chocolates are mine."

"The bear claw is for me?" Zeke asked with a frown.

"Thought it fitting since you growled like one on the phone," I replied before stuffing my trap with a big bite out of each. "Whaff fid you find ouff abouff Boffy?"

"So much for sparkling breakfast conversation."

I swallowed. "Hey, you're the one who ordered and received a free breakfast."

"But I don't like bear claws."

"Too bad." I took a smaller bite. "Can we get back to Bobby please?"

In my experience, most guys will eat anything you place in front of them. Zeke was no exception.

After grousing like a ten year old, he got down to business around a bite of bear claw. "Bobby was arrested late last night."

"Tell me something I don't know. Why?"

"For his wife's murder."

"That's ridiculous," I exclaimed. "Bobby's not a murderer."

"I'm only the messenger."

"But why do they think *Bobby* killed her?"

"Because they discovered an empty bottle of that sleep-aid found in Amy's system sitting in his curbside trash."

Yesterday's events replayed over in my mind, but I couldn't recall seeing any sort of bottles during my cursory glance into the bedrooms.

'Course, I hadn't gone through the trouble of digging into their cabinets or anything. Why would I? They'd barely moved into the house before Amy's death.

The curb had held a myriad of boxes when I'd pulled up and more by the time I'd left. I scanned the memory banks of my gray matter again.

Nope, no medicine bottles.

"There were a ton of moving boxes by the curb by the time I left yesterday," I mused. "Anyone could've simply driven by and added an assortment of crap to the pile."

"True," Zeke said.

"The real murderer could've planted it."

"It's possible."

It didn't make sense. We were out there together most of the day. Bobby never acted like he had anything to hide. Matter of fact, he'd been pretty open about Amy's family background when I'd asked him about it.

He hadn't said anything about the police contacting him again either. So what had changed?

"When did the police reopen the case?" I asked.

"Yesterday."

"But why'd they go after Bobby?"

Zeke didn't hesitate. "Apparently you asked too many questions that didn't have adequate answers."

"Wait a minute," I said, taking the time to chew and swallow the last of my donut while I wrapped my brain around what Zeke *didn't* say. "You're blaming me for Bobby's arrest?"

He tossed back the dregs of coffee like a shot of Jack. "You do have a tendency to get people into trouble."

I didn't even have to work up a glare at that and wished daggers would come shooting out of my eyes into his rock hard, beckoning chest.

The empty coffee cup cracked as I smashed it down on the countertop and turned to leave in a huff. Zeke's firm grip didn't allow me to get very far.

"Would it help to know what I think?"

I didn't trust myself at the moment and shrugged instead of allowing my disease-ridden mouth to take over the conversation.

In my silence, Zeke continued. "I think the police acted far too rashly by arresting Bobby on such thin, circumstantial evidence. This isn't gonna stick without hard proof. And for the record? No, I don't think Bobby's a murderer."

"Really?" The flame of my anger tempered. "So what *do* you believe?"

"That there's someone out there who wants us to think he is."

Guilty or innocent, there's something so wrong about walking into the lockup.

It's like a sense of guilt by association. Like they're never gonna let you leave once you step past the gates and hear that ominous clang when they slam the doors shut.

I had no idea what all Zeke had told them when he called to clear the path for me to visit Bobby, though I wouldn't put it past him to have me booked on drunk and disorderly for some past infraction.

Was there a statute on slapping a cheating ex-boyfriend?

With dark circles under deer-in-the-headlight eyes, Bobby looked like death warmed over. Blond hair stood at all angles like he'd spent the night fisting it in frustration.

His tall frame slumped into a chair on the other side of the glass, while the accompanying guard held the wall up behind him like he had a rod up his, er – spine.

If the situation weren't so dire, it would've made me laugh to think the squat guard could've stood a chance against his charge. Physically Bobby was present, but I couldn't say the same for his mental state.

"I'm at a loss, Vic," Bobby mumbled into the two-way speakerphone. "Why is this happening?"

"Don't worry, Bobby," I soothed. "I'm here for you. So is Zeke. He's checking into all this right now."

That brought Bobby's glazed eyes to mine. "Zeke's helping me?"

I nodded. "Neither of us believe the charges against you. Zeke said it's probably some overzealous atheistic idiot at the DA's office, 'specially if all they've got is that empty medicine bottle from your curbside trash."

"I've been sitting here all night wondering if this is how Jesus felt when He was wrongly accused."

Leave it to Bobby to tie circumstances to the spiritual. Just as long as we didn't have a crucifixion or a giant earthquake that loosed his chains and opened the jail doors, we'd be fine.

"When do you go before the judge for preliminaries?" I asked.

"Sometime later this morning."

"No worries then. Your parents will cover whatever bond is set, and you'll be out of here by noon."

"*If* they will," Bobby responded. "After the phone call in the middle of the night, I haven't heard or seen hide nor hair of them."

"Wait," I said. "They haven't even visited you?"

"Nope. Likely they've spent the night in a committee conference discussing damage control."

"Damage control?"

"For the ministry. The media's gonna have a field day, you know."

The shock of realization hit me like a bucket of ice-cold beer on wet t-shirt night. "Damn the media! You're their son."

Bobby sighed. "Now you see why I've rarely seen eye-to-eye with them. It's their ministry expectations above all else…including me."

"Then I'll take care of bail."

"With what?"

"I'll…I'll…," I started before I could bring myself to say the words. "I'll go into hock. Sell my soul and my body. Grovel on my knees at my dad's feet if I have to."

"Can't let you do that, Vic."

"Hey, as long as you show up for court, Frankie'll get his money back. Or when they drop these ridiculous charges."

"Still can't let you do that," he said. "You and your dad are like warriors with endless supplies of hand grenades and ammo. One of you would end up dead and the other in here with me before I even went to trial."

He had a point. "Then we gotta get them to drop the charges."

"Easier said than done. Unless…"

I could almost hear the wheels loosen and begin to turn in Bobby's brain as thought processes ramped back up from the stresses of a night in the slammer. A light gleamed in his eyes. His jaw set.

"Yeah?" I prompted to loosen his tongue.

"There's a key to my house hidden in a clay pot near the garage. Do you think you could get inside?"

"Sure. What do you need me to look for?"

"Those boxes in the spare bedroom where you changed. Some of them were from Amy's mom that we never got around to sorting through."

"I thought you dragged them all to the curb."

"Not those," Bobby murmured. "I hadn't decided whether to get rid of them yet."

Ah-ha. The half-hearted greeting. The makeshift football. The bad attitude.

"Are they what had you all knotted up when I got there yesterday?"

Bobby nodded. "And there's something in 'em you need to see."

CHAPTER FIFTEEN

Mom always said a lady never sweats. She glistens.

Seems God forgot that tidbit when He hardwired my endocrine system, 'cause I can sweat just as much as Pastor Dennis during a holy roller revival. I read somewhere once that it's not the heat but the humidity.

That moron apparently never visited central Texas in June.

And was probably male. They like to sweat, you know.

Think about it.

While Zeke spent the day in his cool comfortable office, poking around the periphery of a Dallas PD case, I spent the afternoon parked up the next street behind a row of boxwood, waiting for a chance to enter Bobby's modest home.

Quite a far cry from the Vernet estate across town, that's for sure.

I got a good look at Bobby's place this time. Tan siding. Brick façade on the lower half. Standard two-car garage we'd successfully made a dent in the day before. What I'd seen inside the house was pretty cookie-cutter for this subdivision.

'Cept for the view through the big picture window. Officers crawled around inside and ducked under yellow crime scene tape wrapped around the outside like a package expressed from Santa Claus.

All this for an empty bottle of sleeping pills? Talk about overkill.

"Are you okay, dear?"

The question from the neighbor startled me in my half-asleep state. It's really hard to stay conscious when your day starts way too early and the heat sends you into a catatonic state. That, and the fact I really had to pee after downing my third coke.

I blinked then recognized Nosy Nana from this week's exciting adventure of *Unpacking with Bobby*. Coifed gray hair was teased high like a coil of cotton candy at the state fair. The bright pink nylon wind suit sold the appearance of an afternoon out for a walk.

Seeing it just made me sweat all the more.

"I'm fine," I mumbled, wiping sleep-induced drool from the corner of my mouth.

"Oh, I recognize you now," Nosy Nana proclaimed. "You were over yesterday helping out the young pastor who lives next door."

"Yeah, I'm a family friend."

Nana shook her head. "Such a sweet thing, his wife. Sure is a shame what happened."

She gave me the *look*.

You know the one I'm talking about. That direct stare with eyebrows raised in expectation and a mouth crossed between a smile and surprised shock.

So fake. So earnest for information she could spread around like the ranking member of Gossipers 'R Us.

I was so not in the mood to deal with her.

"Well, you know what they say...don't believe everything you hear," I practically snarled. "There's more to the story than what the Neighborhood Watch and Gossip Committee is saying."

The comment got me a purse of orange-red lips and a sniff before she took up the trot again, arms swinging and butt jiggling like two trapped cats fighting for supremacy.

Told you I could be bitchy when I didn't get enough sleep.

I rubbed my forehead, took another sip of warm and watered-down pop, then punched in Zeke's number on my cell.

"What now, Vicki?"

"Why's Bobby's house been crawling with cops all day?"

A pause. "Please tell me you're not attempting a stakeout."

"I thought those were at night. What're they called in the middle of the day?"

"Stay away from his house, Vic."

"It's not like I meant to hang here all afternoon, but the cops won't leave and Bobby asked me to check on something."

"Don't tell me you have a key to his house now."

"I do not."

"No wait...he told you which rock to look under for the spare."

I hesitated. "Maybe."

The sigh came out more like a growl. "Look, I'm only gonna say this once," Zeke grumbled. "Stay away from the crime scene."

"But no crime was committed here. Why're they blocking it off?"

"They found evidence there that may have been used in a crime."

"It was on the curb," I countered.

"Which leads a good investigator to dig deeper and check the house."

"Whose side are you on here?"

"It's what I'd do in their shoes," Zeke said. "Especially considering the extremely weak evidence they've collected so far. They're gonna need more than an empty bottle found at the curb to make the DA's case against Bobby stick."

"But what about when Bobby gets home?" I asked.

"That might be awhile. His bail was set pretty high."

"For a bottle of sleeping pills? What about his parents?"

"No one's shown up to bond him out yet," Zeke confessed. "It's going on four o'clock, so without a miracle he'll probably have to wait until tomorrow."

The thought of Bobby spending another night in jail about made me sick. Or maybe it was the heat.

I wanted to drive right over to the Vernet mansion, blast through their gates, then grab Mary Jo by her skinny little neck and wring it like a chicken. How dare a mother abandon her child. May as well have sentenced him to death.

The image of a pregnant Amy splayed out in a parking lot popped into my mind. Ouch!

"So what now?" I finally asked.

"There's nothing else to do today. Now go home, clean up, and get ready for work tonight."

Work – oh, crap. In all the distractions I'd almost forgotten what day it was.

Janine would be out of classes soon and calling again for an update if I didn't catch her first. I could come back to Bobby's house later tonight after I got off work.

When it wasn't invaded by cops.
When it was quiet.
Dark.
Didn't Zeke say stakeouts were usually at night?
Oh yeah. That was me.

Yellow crime scene tape glowed under the muted cast of streetlights and fluttered like a specter signaling *beware of the haunted house.*

'Course I don't believe in spooks. Or spirits.

I think.

Imagination ignored, I crept in the shadows around the side of Bobby's garage then plucked the key from the fake rock nestled in the terra cotta urn.

Why do people do that? You know, put a key to their house inside an obvious fake rock right out in the open. It's fooling nobody. Instead it's pretty much an advertisement to thieves like a billboard publicizing a free-for-all flea market bonanza inside someone's house – *Everything Must Go!*

If I ever owned a house I'd just dig a hole and bury the key in the garden. Then again, knowing me, I'd probably dig too deep. Forget where I buried it.

Oh, like you could do better!

Sneaking around to the rear porch, I spied a strip of yellow tape at the back door. One end was floating like a streamer left over from a backyard birthday barbeque.

As I entered the house, I reminded myself the whole walk across the living room that I had permission to be there. All Nosy Nana had to do, if she was up at this hour for a pee run, was to ask Bobby.

Once he was bailed out of jail, of course.

After shutting out the late night cicada serenade and making my way upstairs, I stood at the top of the staircase and listened to the silence. What was once on its way to being a happy home felt heavy and oppressive without life pulsating between the walls.

No husband snoring down the hall.

No pregnant wife up emptying her overwrought bladder or for a three A.M. feeding.

No baby's cry.

Maybe Bobby was better off spending another night in the slammer than here with the memories of what should've been.

With the dark piece of plastic bag secured over the flashlight, soft illumination revealed the spare bedroom. Once neatly stacked blue t-shirts were scattered. Box contents were dumped across the bed and on the floor. A slashed mattress propped against the wall with box springs askew.

It didn't look so much like police had searched for anything – more like they'd released a Texas-sized tornado.

Well, my job just got harder.

I tipped a box upright then shoved in t-shirts until they were out of the way. After setting that box in the hallway, I grabbed another and sat down on the floor to begin the real work.

"The things I go through for friends," I grumbled.

An hour later I wished for my bed. Which made me wish for Nick. Which made me think of Ford F-150s. Which made me remember in whose house I was.

Which woke me up enough to realize what I held in my hand.

"Well hello," I murmured. "Where've you been all night?"

The hand-carved humidor was beautiful even in the diffused light, the patina at the edges caused by the oils of skin touching it over years of opening and closing. A cache of envelopes yellowed with age spilled across the lined interior while the faint scent of tobacco tickled my nose.

The scent reminded me of visits to Louisiana with Janine when we were girls. It smelled like her grandfather when he'd hug us.

If my olfactory memory served, we weren't talking just any cigar. The best of the best. This humidor once contained Gurkha's His Majesty's Reserve.

At nearly a thousand dollars a stogie, we're talking some serious coin, folks.

How did Amy's mom come to own a humidor that had once contained some of the most expensive cigars in the world?

The only reason it was still here was because the police who'd searched this room earlier probably had no clue how much the humidor alone was worth. Which meant they couldn't have cared less about the aged and yellowed letters either.

The envelope on top appeared disturbed, the letter peeking out from beneath the fold as if haphazardly shoved inside. Unsigned love notes from an admirer.

The officers had probably had a good laugh after perusing the first few. The ones underneath remained undisturbed – until I got to the bottom.

The flap was cracked. I unfolded the missive to discover the lone letter with a signature, a name Bobby hadn't dared speak aloud over the jail phone.

Amy's father wasn't just any Tom, Dick, or Harry. I stared at the signature of one Julio Benito Juarez – the current Mexican Ambassador to the United States.

My whistle of surprise changed to a squeak with the press of metal against the back of my skull and an unfamiliar male voice in my ear.

"Hands up."

CHAPTER SIXTEEN

There's something to be said for having friends in high places. In this case, law enforcement.

"Victoria Bohanan. Any relation to..."

"Distantly," I said with only a hint of an eye roll.

'Course I didn't tell Detective Horace Duncan the distance between me and my father was merely symbolic. We lived in the same town, but we may as well have lived on separate planets.

But I digress.

When the detective dragged my sorry carcass from Bobby's house before sunrise tinged the sky pink, I should've been scared beyond all reason. I was dead. Headed to the slammer if I couldn't sweet talk my way out of this one. Soon to become someone's unwilling bitch.

But there's something about pulling an all-nighter that causes my sanity to go the way of the rotary phone.

Or maybe it had more to do with Duncan's surly attitude as he shoved me through the front doors of the precinct.

Rumpled cheap suit, balding dome, and a greasy complexion in the early-morning mugginess wasn't nearly as bad as the stench of Old Spice in the close confines of the interrogation room. Hard dark eyes swept over and through me like I was a mere apparition.

'Cept when they settled for too long below my neck.

Since arriving on this side of puberty, I'd had many a man stare and talk to the endowments God chose to *bless* me with. For some, I didn't mind accentuating the positives. For others, I didn't care for the slimy optical undressing.

Duncan fit firmly into the *others* category, though I was inclined to dislike him on first sight. Not to mention that he hadn't let me have my one phone call yet.

"Didn't you see the police tape, Miss Bohanan?"

"Was that what that was?" I asked, playing all ditzy and wide-eyed innocent.

Trust me. Acting wasn't all that easy for a smart and sophisticated gal like me.

Oh, shut up.

"Can you read?"

"Not in the dark."

Duncan reached into his pocket, pulled out a roll, and unwound a short section. "Can you read it now?"

"Po-lice line," I repeated, trying to keep up pretenses. "Do. Not. Cross."

"Which you did."

"No, I didn't."

"What do you call it then?"

I pointed. "That particular piece of tape wasn't there."

That got me a purse of thin lips. "But some just like it was."

"Says you."

"And a whole investigative crew," the detective returned. "It means you do not go under it."

"I didn't go under it," I countered. "The only thing I saw near the back door was a yellow streamer with one end attached to the house and another end floating in the breeze like a windsock."

Duncan cricked his neck. "Under, over, around or through…you don't cross a police line."

"Can you take these things off?" I asked, jiggling my cuffed hands in his face. "They're cutting into my wrists, and boy howdy, you do not want my boss seeing bruises on me. He gets a mite upset when people hurt the help."

Duncan's fist jostled the table and vibrated the glass partition. "You weren't just breaking and entering, but breaking and entering a *crime scene*."

"I didn't break anything. I actually tidied up a bit after the mess you guys made. And I had permission to be there."

"Permission? From who?"

"The homeowner. And I had a key."

"You mean this thing?" He flung the key onto the table. "It's still not a get out of jail free card."

I tried another tack. "Don't you guys record all inmate conversations?"

"What's that got to do with…?"

"Mr. Vernet specifically asked me to find something for him."

"What do you fancy yourself? Some private investigator? Nancy Drew?"

"Just someone helping out a friend is all."

"In case you didn't know, PI's are required to be licensed. You're just some bartender babe."

"Hey, I have a B.A.," I responded with a little heat.

"In what? Bad-Assery?"

"Business, dumb-ass."

"So why're you wasting it bartending?" Duncan asked.

"Maybe I'm planning to open my own place someday. Use those business skills I earned in college."

He leaned forward, his stare dipping again below my neck. "So why were you at my crime scene?"

"Like I said, helping a friend."

"Clearing evidence of his crime, you mean." Duncan ran a finger over the edge of the humidor.

"Bobby Vernet didn't kill his wife! Why don't you do a little investigating and actually listen to our conversation from this morning...er, yesterday morning," I challenged.

"Because I already did." A smirk planted firmly on his face just before a knock at the interrogation door. "How do you think I found you?"

When Duncan opened the door, I felt like the head football coach getting the Gatorade bath at the end of the game. Only this time I wasn't on the winning team.

Tired eyes held restrained flames of fury only waiting to be unleashed. "Duncan," Zeke greeted.

"Taylor," the detective responded, an unnaturally gleeful grin on his face.

Out of the frying pan and into the fire. I was about to be someone's bitch alright.

Yup, I was so dead.

Silence.

I wasn't about to be the one to break it. With no sleep for the past twenty-four hours and only one cup of coffee flowing through my veins, synapses weren't firing in my brain.

None of which boded well for a woman struggling against a relapse of foot-in-mouth disease.

Instead I listened to the rumble of Zeke's Ford Raptor and watched the sun rise over a new day in Dallas.

The day Ranger Taylor saved my sorry carcass from rotting in a Dallas jail cell.

The day my account balance with Zeke went so deep into the negative I was swimming in red. He owned my hide.

And we both knew it.

"I told you to stay away," he finally growled.

"Well, you can see how that didn't work," I responded.

"Why won't you ever listen to me?"

"Bobby needed me to…"

My body jerked against the seatbelt as Zeke slammed on the brakes with a squeal of molten tires and slid the truck onto the highway shoulder in one tug of the steering wheel.

The stench of burned rubber filled the cab. Horns honked and fingers were offered up in the southern salute, but Zeke's attention was all on me.

"Are you ready to join him in *jail*?"

"All Bobby wanted me to do was see those letters," I huffed.

"Will you listen to yourself? Bobby this and Bobby that. Do you know how close you were to being booked?"

In a moment of clarity and wisdom, I found it best to exercise my right to remain silent.

Zeke took a deep breath and pulled back out onto the road. "Damnit, Vic, I'm trying to help you here. But you've gotta start helping yourself by listening to me for once in your life. You're not gonna do Bobby any good sitting right beside him."

Too bad I didn't have the ability to remain silent for long.

"Then what should I have done all day? Wait around for you to finish planning security for the governor's visit?"

"If I'd known what you were looking for, I could've made a phone call. Arranged to meet up with Duncan at the house after I got off work."

"Would you have let me go inside with you?" I asked pointedly.

"It's an active crime scene," was all Zeke said.

"Then I'd have never gotten the name of Amy's dad."

Zeke stopped sermonizing for a second. "Is Juarez really her father?"

"I'd say it's a safe bet."

We remained silent until Zeke pulled up in front of my apartment building.

"What about my Vette?" I asked.

"I've taken care of your car. Should be dropped off by ten."

"I guess that means I'll have to stay awake until then," I muttered, dragging my ragged rump from the cab as every wasted hour finally caught up with me.

Zeke rolled down the window after I shut the door. "Remember, I'm still working on things from my end. I don't want to see an innocent man in jail any more than you."

My brain was rapidly shutting down. "Yeah, yeah."

"I mean it, Vicki. Call me if you need me for *anything*."

If my antenna hadn't been so addled, I'd have suspected more lingered behind Zeke's statement than an intent to help with Bobby's situation.

The truck idled at the curb while the roving ranger waited for me to enter my complex, stumble past the super's apartment, and up the stairs. In my present state, the only male I'd allow in my rumpled bed was my ball-less and claw-less tabby.

After all, a girl needed sleep on occasion, right folks?

Ever have one of those headaches from lack of sleep?

It's different from the piercing headache caused from a hangover, where light and sound are like a hot poker to the gray matter. It's the kind of ache where your brain feels too heavy for your skull. Disembodied and fuzzy.

When you've got one of those, it takes far too much effort to piece together a single sentence, much less follow through on any action.

The tequila bottle rested in my hand as I tried to remember if I'd actually poured it in the bar glass a second ago or if I'd dreamt it. I tossed in a measure – just in case – threw a lime wedge on the edge and called it good.

Music warbled around me as if coming from a tin can. Thank God the bar remained slow tonight.

After spending the eventful morning with Duncan and then Zeke, a nap had sounded like the perfect fix to a not-so-perfect day's start. But after collapsing into my bed and drifting faster than a racecar at Daytona, Janine's call for updates got my brain going again – however briefly – as I relayed my visit to Bobby's home and my almost trip to the slammer.

Certain discoveries I'd kept to myself, namely the probability of the chromosomal contribution to Amy's genetic makeup. If it'd concerned Bobby enough not to reveal the name through a recorded jail line, it'd behoove me to hold it close as well and avoid revealing it to outsiders.

"Well now, if it isn't my favorite mind reader."

The familiar voice snapped my brain awake so fast it almost gave me whiplash. "Hey there, Radioman."

Cornflower-blue eyes sparked with interest in the ambient lighting. The amber hair sported the perpetual indentation from wearing headphones all day.

Yeah, I'd love a chance to fix it by ruffling my fingers through it. Or tousle it when he kissed me.

Oh hell, why not just fisting it as he made wild and passionate love to me? With that silky and sultry voice, I'd let him talk dirty to me all night long.

Nope, I no longer felt tired at all. In fact, just call me the energizer bunny.

Radioman chuckled. "Where'd that moniker come from?"

I popped the lid off a Sam Adams and handed it over. "I made it up the night we first met when you came in with your two buddies."

After a long pull, he sat down on a stool. "It's better than Bruce, that's for sure."

"As long as your last name isn't Banner or Wayne, and you don't go running around in the night all green and enraged or caped and cowled, we'll call it good."

"You can call me whatever you want," he growled with a smile.

My legs got a little noodley, and I leaned against the counter to stay upright, even though all my happy-happy hormones wanted to go horizontal.

"What brings you out without the entourage?"

He leaned forward and rested his elbows on either side of his beer. "The chance to see a lovely lady again."

I followed suit and leaned near, loose strands of hair tumbling over my shoulders and pooling on the bar. "Are you flirting with me, Mr. Radioman?"

"I might be." He wound a strand around his finger and gave it a test tug. "You free tomorrow night?"

The spicy scent of his cologne wafted beneath my nostrils as he came in closer for the kill, licking his lips and lowering his lids to half-mast. I sucked in a breath in anticipation of tangled tongues and naughty nipping.

"No, she's not free," Grady interrupted. "She's a working girl."

Exhaustion washed over me again. Radioman pulled away to a more respectable distance – damnit – as Grady sidled up behind and draped an arm across my shoulders like a dog marking his territory.

Pheromones flew thick before I shimmied out from underneath the boss's arm, grabbed a towel, and started taking my frustrations out on the counter.

"Sorry," I muttered. "But yeah, I'm working tomorrow."

Radioman wasn't so easily deterred. "What about another night this week?"

"She's gonna be out of town," another familiar voice called out.

Zeke flanked Radioman, set his black Stetson aside and tapped the bar in front of him. I knew what it meant, but I ignored him on principle and fumed instead.

"What do you mean, I'm gonna be out of town?" I groused.

Grady poured a dark ale from the tap and set it before Ranger Taylor. "Need some alone time with your girl, Zeke?"

"I'm not his girl."

"If it's not too much trouble, Grady," Zeke responded.

"I'm not his girl," I corrected again for Radioman's benefit.

"How many days you gonna need her?" Grady asked Zeke.

"I'm standing right here, guys."

"Tomorrow's all," Zeke continued, completely ignoring me.

Radioman's head toggled back and forth through the ridiculous conversation, quietly drinking his beer and seeming to enjoy the show about me that didn't include me. The slight lift at the corners of his mouth said he was actually relishing my pain.

Men.

"Then how about you give me Saturday night off?" I asked Grady.

"Didn't I just give you a Saturday off?"

"That was for church."

"Then why're you asking for another one so soon?" the boss asked.

"Cause church isn't for fun." I offered up a sultry smile and a wink to Radioman. "That's what dates are for."

Zeke snorted. "Is she always this disrespectful of authority?" he asked Grady.

"Who's being disrespectful?"

"Pretty much."

"Now just a cotton-pickin' minute!" I yelled and pointed a finger in Grady's face. "You won't give me a night off to go on a date, but Ranger Boy, who by the way is *not* my boyfriend," I clarified for Radioman's sake, "comes waltzing in and you give me the night off to spend in *his* company? No questions asked?"

Grady shrugged. "He wouldn't ask if it wasn't important. Besides, you've been so grumpy tonight I figured you could use some entertainment."

"Depends on who's doing the entertaining," I muttered then confronted Zeke. "What's so damn urgent that you need to take away my earning potential?"

"Need you to take a trip down to Austin with me."

"Austin? Why the hell would I need to go to Austin?"

Zeke guzzled the ale and stood, sliding his hat from the bar to his head in one smooth motion – and ignoring my question completely.

"I'll pick you up at seven."

"Seven?" I asked his retreating figure.

"As in A.M."

"In the flippin' morning?"

"Yup."

Grady and Radioman smiled at me in unison. My brain simply glazed over. Too many early mornings in a row.

Would someone just shoot me?

CHAPTER SEVENTEEN

"Don't talk to me," I muttered, squinting behind my sunglasses and ducking beneath the ball cap bill to avoid the early morning sun.

Might as well call me a vampire 'cause at this rate I'd shrivel up the moment the rays touched any part of my physiology. Early mornings and I have never gone together in any sphere, universe, or alternate dimension. I'm a mistress of the night.

In more ways than one, right?

"Good morning to you too," Zeke offered as I swept by him and stormed across the parking lot to his extended cab.

When I tried to open the door, resistance sent me reeling toward the asphalt until Zeke stopped my backward progress. Arms I'd once found delightful wrapped around my body.

But not anymore.

Like an inebriated date, I jerked from his embrace and stumbled against the frame. The click of locks hardly concealed Zeke's chuckle as he peeled me aside and opened the truck door.

"Asshole," I muttered, inspecting a couple of broken nails.

"Coffee's on the dash."

That sent me scrambling up into the truck faster than you could say *chocolate*.

I barely tasted the brew until I'd drained over half the extra-large cup, and Zeke had us dodging traffic along I-35 headed south. With my brain beginning the journey toward semi-consciousness, I checked around the floor and console.

"What? No breakfast?"

Zeke threw a glance over his shoulder before nudging between two rigs barreling down the left lane. It felt like we were a soft, gooey center about to be smashed between two hard cookies ala Oreo.

"I wanna get clear of the worst of this mess first," Zeke said. "We'll stop at a café between Hillsboro and Waco."

"Oh huh-uh. I know what *between* means to you, Zeke Taylor. If you don't want your precious truck wearing a revisit of the coffee I've already swallowed, you will not make me wait 'til Waco."

"Lean back and take a nap then."

"After drinking an extra-large Big Z special blend that's strong enough to rot a hole through my empty gut?"

"Why'd you drink the damn thing so fast?" Zeke punctuated his frustration with a sharp mash to the brake to avoid sliding beneath the leading rig's undercarriage.

I braced against the dash to keep from becoming road kill. "Because with the way you drive, it'd end up wasted on the floorboards otherwise."

"Before or after the revisit?"

"I need food!" I demanded. "Sooner would be better than later."

Mutterings punctuated with a word or two unfit for feminine ears emanated from the driver's seat. Taking a brief opening in traffic, Zeke weaved the Raptor to the right between a flashy little Lexus and an RV on its last lug nut.

A couple of miles down the road, and he'd successfully maneuvered into the far right-hand lane to exit near the great metropolis of Italy, Texas.

The truck stop sat at the edge of no-man's land. The only thing that stared back at us – besides livestock – was an enormous sign large enough for the International Space Station to read Earth's current gas prices and a great big, yellow M.

"Oh hell no," I exclaimed. "You are not taking me to eat at that Mickey D's."

"Well I sure as hell ain't sittin' here waitin' for the steakhouse to open for lunch," Zeke responded as he pulled into a parking spot and shut off the engine. "It's the golden arches now or you can wait until Waco, princess."

The loud protestations of my belly cinched it. Grumblings of frustration joined those of my hollow portions as I climbed from the truck and punctuated my irritation by slamming the door before stomping into what was loosely referred to as a restaurant.

See why I don't get up before ten? I'm usually a nice human being. Honest. It's just multiple early mornings in a row with little more than a couple of hours sleep in between left me severely depleted. The bitchy needle was firmly lodged in the red zone.

Then there was the whole thing with Bobby in jail for murder hanging over my head. Couple that with spending an entire day in the presence of my ex-boyfriend.

Can I get a little sympathy now?

Two heart attack platters and a couple of scorching-hot coffees later, Zeke and I launched back onto the interstate, heading south toward our goal. *Our* goal? Hmm.

A reasonably comfortable tummy and a bloodstream pumping with enough caffeine to put down a rhino had awakened me enough to ask some reasonably non-bitchy questions.

"I guess I should've inquired earlier, but why exactly am I going with you to Austin?"

Traffic had grown a bit more reasonable and so had Zeke, all slouched in the seat with his Stetson pushed back, one arm resting lazily on the steering wheel and the other on the seat between us.

In the old days, I'd have been in that spot where his hand sat. Or propped on the edge of his lap. Or in his lap.

My pulse took a slight uptick at the memory. Maybe it was the caffeine flood.

Yeah, that'll work.

"Gotta job for you," Zeke said.

"Better not be a blow job," I mumbled.

He grinned. "We'll save that for later."

"Ain't gonna be a later when I leap from this cab."

"Grab what's between your legs."

"Excuse me?" My squeak could've cracked the windshield.

"Lord Almighty, woman. Underneath the seat."

Who was bitchy now?

I reached beneath the seat and produced a soft-sided brown briefcase. Well, what do you know? Zeke Taylor, Mr. Cowboy Extraordinaire, carried a briefcase.

I chuckled. Then I cracked up. Warm tears trickled down my cheeks and my abs felt like they'd endured too many crunches before laughter subsided.

Maybe it was the sleepy sillies. "When did you start getting so important you had to get a briefcase?"

"Just hand it over." Zeke pointed to the seat between us. "I always carry one when I have to travel."

"Brown doesn't match your hat or truck," I observed.

"I didn't want a hard case, and this one only came in brown."

With his knee in the driving position and one eye on the road, Zeke rummaged through the case. A glance through a couple of folders, then he pulled out a manila envelope from one.

Zeke has an incredible poker face. It's what makes him so good at his job. It also makes him a formidable opponent in the card game. When we'd dated, he was the Company 'B' Ranger Station poker champion.

Played for the prestige, folks. No money changed hands.

But when you get personal and in touch with every inch of someone – and I mean *every* inch – you pick up on more than just physical tells. You can feel it when something's not right.

"What's all that?" I asked, pointing at the briefcase full of folders.

"*My* job," Zeke grunted, handing me the envelope.

"Oka-a-ay, what's this?"

"*Your* job," he explained. "While I'm hammering out some security details about the governor's visit next week, you're gonna have a pow-wow with the vital statistics office."

"Vital statistics? You mean like birth and death certificates? Marriage and divorces?"

"Yup."

I stared at the envelope in my hands then up at Zeke. "You're not getting any weird ideas here, are you?"

"Just look through the damn envelope."

A signed waiver from Bobby. A court order authorizing a search of Amy's records.

I shivered. "Amy's birth and death records?"

"Stick with the birth record," Zeke commanded. "We both know how she died."

That shut me up tighter than a sinner on Sunday.

I'm not sure how much sleep I got, but when I peeked through one slit to see a myriad of state government offices, I knew we'd arrived in Austin – minus my skull.

A short nap when the need was so great left my body begging for more and amplified the misery. It would've been better if I hadn't succumbed to Mr. Sandman.

A sweaty bottle of Dr. Pepper clouded my vision. "Rise and shine, princess. Take this dripping caffeine fix before I toss it."

"You always know how to sweet talk a girl," I grumbled and took a swig.

"It's a good thing I know what you want when you wake. I need you on this side of human for a few hours."

Under normal circumstances, what I wanted when I awoke next to a good ol' hunk of man flesh wasn't fit to speak aloud. Or write in print.

But considering the man beside me was my ex-boyfriend and a lying, scum-sucking cheater, I had no trouble restraining myself.

Cross my heart.

Plus, there was the fact we were in his truck cab. And it was daylight. I have some standards after all.

Oh, be quiet.

As I added caffeine to my bloodstream, I flipped through the envelope's contents again. "Okay, tell me again why I'm here."

"You need a copy of Amy's birth certificate and any accompanying documentation."

I slid the authorization from the envelope. "Wanna tell me how you got Bobby's signature?"

Zeke shrugged. "Went to the jail."

"Wait," I exclaimed. "Wait, wait, wait. So you're telling me Bobby's parents *still* haven't bonded him out?"

"They're not exactly in a position to front a five hundred thousand dollar bond."

"But their house…"

"Is mortgaged to the hilt and they're upside down," Zeke said.

"But…" I stopped. "Hold on a sec. How do you know that?"

"I know."

"But how?" I prodded.

"Look, I know we aren't seeing each other anymore, but can you for once just trust me without having to know every single detail?"

"Fine."

"Good."

Zeke parked the truck in the ensuing silence, exited his side, then opened the door for me like a gentleman while I finished making myself presentable. The wave of heat off the pavement sucked the air from my lungs.

How was it possible a mere two hundred miles could vary the temperature so much?

"I still have a question," I ventured as Zeke helped me from the truck.

"What is it then?" he asked, running his hand through his hair like he wanted to yank handfuls from the roots.

"You went through the trouble of getting all this paperwork for a simple copy of a birth certificate. But that still doesn't explain why you need little ol' me to traipse in there instead of you. There's a catch here somewhere, and I'm too tired to figure it out, so spill."

"This is a Dallas PD matter, not a Ranger one. You saw how Duncan acted yesterday about someone showing up at his crime scene."

"Like a dog protecting the last morsel on his bone."

"Exactly. A random murder isn't under Ranger jurisdictional mandate. However, drug smuggling is."

"Drug smuggling? But Amy wasn't doing drugs. Her mother was..." The caffeine hit my brain and jumpstarted it in time for me to put two-and-two together to get four instead of five. "You're investigating a drug ring, aren't you?"

"Prudence and the confidential nature of the case requires I keep my mouth shut and not say anything." Instead Zeke offered a curt nod and tap to his nose.

"You suspect there's a tie-in between your case and Amy's death then?"

"Hypothetically speaking," Zeke started. "At minimum a circumstantial link will allow me to join the murder investigation. At best I can pull rank, but that won't do anything to keep me in Duncan's good graces."

"I'm beginning to see some method to your madness. But it still doesn't explain why you need *me* to help you."

Zeke sighed. "As big a pain in my ass as you can be sometimes, you've always possessed good observational skills. Been able to read people and see between the lines, even though you have an uncanny ability to misconstrue the obvious."

"Um, thanks...I think?"

"Start small. Ask to see the birth records. Get copies. Then see where it takes you." Zeke tapped the envelope in my hands. "If you need more, documents in there will give you access to every record they've got." He leaned over and kissed the top of my head. "I'll see you in a couple of hours."

I stood in the middle of the oven-like parking lot getting high on asphalt fumes as Zeke swung up into his truck and drove away. I'm not sure which shocked me more – the kiss on the head or the roundabout compliment.

I blame the asphalt fumes.

CHAPTER EIGHTEEN

Have you ever noticed something about a lot of low-level government employees? Most of them are lacking in even the most basic customer service skills. And they have no hitch in their giddyup.

I wonder if it's something in the water. Maybe recruiters look for a certain attitude in their handy-dandy hiring evaluations. All I know is anytime I've ever dealt with one, all I get is little help and plenty of insolence.

It isn't me – is it?

Don't answer that.

Like an obedient and mindless worker ant, I took a position at the end of the line from hell and shuffled forward a half inch with each passing minute.

After an interminable wait, I finally bellied up to the counter and secured a copy of Amy's birth certificate without fuss. I felt like pressing the easy button until a quick glance revealed no one referenced as father and the word *amended* in bold caps at the top.

Before the next constituent reached the counter, I forced my way back in. The greasy guy bumped into me with his beer gut before conceding the space.

I hoped my shirt had avoided a skid mark. "Um, this copy says the birth certificate was amended."

The squat lady behind the counter didn't even look at me. "Means there was a change to the record. I can help the next person."

"Okay," I continued, keeping Beer Gut at bay. "But I need a copy of the original."

"That *is* the original. Next!"

Beer Gut jostled me again and tried to do the bump-n-boogie with my hip. I *accidentally* stepped on his toe with my boot heel.

"No, this is the amended," I insisted, holding up the certificate and pointing to the word.

That got me an eye roll followed by the stare of death over the top of her glasses. At least I had her full attention this time.

"Once amended it is classified as the original."

"Look, I just need a copy of the entire birth record then."

"Listen, honey." The glasses dropped from her nose and cradled between sagging breasts at the end of a glittering lanyard only Lady Gaga could appreciate. "Unless you've got a court order, what you're holding in your prissy little fingers *is* the entire birth record. Next person!"

Oh huh-uh. She did *not* just dismiss me like a two-timing mistress.

With negligible sleep over the past forty-eight hours, a breakfast practically guaranteeing revenge from Montezuma *and* his ancestors, coupled with the last three hours in the company of my ex-boyfriend, Madam Bitchy was going down against Miz Bitchette.

"You want a court order, *honey*?"

I ripped the remaining papers from the envelope, not even slowed by the sting of a paper cut. The slap of my hand on the counter caused Beer Gut to retreat another step as Madam Bitchy's eyes widened.

"Here's your damn court order, complete with judge's signature and the seal of the great State of Texas," I pointed out for emphasis. "Now if it's not too much of a bother to move your ass and do the job my tax dollars are paying you to do, I need a copy of the *entire* record."

That garnered hearty clapping, a couple of hoots, and a *that-a-girl* followed by a gruff *you-show'em* scattered throughout the line.

Ten minutes later and just over a hundred dollars in the hole – something Zeke conveniently forgot to mention I'd have to cover – I sat in the downstairs lobby waiting for my ride.

The envelope was stuffed to overflowing with Amy's records. A cursory search through the mess revealed the certifiable proof we were hoping for in black and white.

Julio Benito Juarez was Amy's father.

While Zeke confiscated my envelope and ran in to speak to the deputy assistant director of the Ranger Corp, I got to sit in another uncomfortable chair.

Only this time it was in the corner of a little café at the Texas Department of Public Safety.

I guess he thought another cup of coffee constituted adequate compensation for my time, not to mention the hundred plus dollars I was out obtaining the desired information.

Hey, I paid for those papers. If Zeke wasn't more forthcoming on the drive home, I had three hours to get in a few words and tell him what I really thought of him.

After nursing my second coffee to stave off the afternoon nods and salivating over the pastry counter, wishing we hadn't missed lunch, Zeke finally made a reappearance. All I needed was one glance to tell me his mood wavered closer to kill than stun.

The discussion over my unexpectedly abused funds could wait until both of us had some proper nourishment. A sharp jerk of his chin had me on his tail faster than you could say jump.

Under normal circumstances, I'm not one of those women who says *how high* when a man says *jump*. I'm more likely to issue a rebuke along the line of *kiss my ass* or better yet, offer the southern salute.

You know, the middle finger?

But after knowing Zeke for so many years, I'd never seen such dark clouds gather so fast or feel the lightning bolts crackle under his skin – and I wasn't about to stand between that cloud-to-ground path. Something big had just exploded with his boss, and Zeke reeked of ozone.

I kept quiet through the silent stalk across the parking lot and even the tire screech as Zeke whipped the truck from the parking lot onto Lamar Boulevard. But when we passed a host of restaurants as we neared the Highway 69 and I-35 interchange at full-throttle, I knew the last thing on the Ranger's mind was food.

Lucky for him he had me in tow. "If you'll just pull into that steakhouse over yonder I'll foot the bill."

Talk about desperate.

The mention of food snapped Zeke out of his dark trance, at least enough to get him to notice the dashboard clock inching toward three. A sheepish brow furrow replaced the scowl.

My navel nearly leapt for joy when the tick of a turn signal broke the silence, and we passed under the interchange to turn right. I could almost taste the sizzling beef when we drove into the restaurant parking lot.

Just what I needed, a big, juicy steak to put me into a coma for the drive to Dallas. As we walked inside, the scents hit my olfactory senses and triggered a demanding rumble from my belly before we were even seated.

"Sorry for leaving you hanging, Vic. I lost all track of time today."

"My stomach thanks you for stopping," I said, muscling my way into a booth faster than you can say *howdy*.

"Get whatcha want then. I'm buying," Zeke offered with a wink.

"I guess chivalry is not dead," I mused and ordered a sampler appetizer platter with our drinks.

A couple of buffalo wings, half the spinach artichoke dip, and most of the cheddar-bacon potato wedges later, I slowed enough to tip-toe around a few issues.

Ah, what the hell. Subtlety has never been my strong suit, so I dove right in instead of wading.

"I take it things didn't go so great today," I said between bites.

The dark scowl threatened to return before a long pull emptied the one beer Zeke allowed when driving. A satisfied sigh relaxed the tension lines around his eyes. It reminded me of the before and after when we'd dated.

You know, before and after the tango between the sheets?

If he'd had a rough day at work, I could melt that stress away before pizza delivery arrived. Afterward we'd enjoy the glow while we ate.

Not sure I liked my ministrations being replaced by a bottle of beer though.

"Morning went well," Zeke offered. "While you were playing Nancy Drew, we got all our ducks aligned for the governor's visit to Dallas next week."

"You've no idea what Nancy Drew went through to get Amy's records."

"Tough crowd?"

"Psycho-controlling clerk stingier with information than Ebenezer Scrooge with money."

Zeke chuckled. "Sorry I missed that bitch-slap fest."

"Speaking of bitch-slapping, you owe me a hundred and two dollars and seventy cents."

Without even batting an eye or asking to see a receipt, Zeke flipped out his wallet and extracted a few twenties. No rebuttal. No sarcasm. No belaboring the issue until steam seeped from my collar.

Where was this guy when we'd dated?

My eyes narrowed when he pushed the cash across the table. "You feeling okay?"

"I'll have to owe you for the two dollars and seventy cents."

"You can write me a check when we get back to Dallas," I said, sliding the twenties toward him.

He shoved it right back to me. "No can do. Can't have a paper trail between me and this case."

"But I thought the point of this trip was…"

"There may be a tie-in between Amy's death and a case I'm working," Zeke whispered.

"I knew it," I responded in kind.

Bitterness tinged his voice as the cloud descended once again. "But the higher-ups don't see it. Frankly, it's more like they don't *want* to see it."

"Can you blame them? With an ambassador involved, it gets kinda tricky."

"And if the State Department, FBI, or DEA get wind of this, they'll have a field day hampering my investigation, that is if they don't swipe it out from underneath me and make it disappear first."

"Well, I guess that's it then."

"What?" Zeke raised a brow in suspicion.

"I want to help Bobby. You have an investigation that needs solved. Somehow these are tied together, so that means you still need my help."

"Oh no. I had a hunch and it didn't play out the way I'd hoped. Thanks for your help today, but when we get back to Dallas it's the end of the road for you."

"I wouldn't count me out just yet."

"I mean it, Vic. Give it up."

I popped a chip in my mouth and smiled just as the waitress brought our entrees to the table. The poor guy wouldn't know what hit him by the time I was through.

Give it up?

I was just getting warmed up.

So much for warming up the bus.

My three beer dinner left me drooling on Zeke's upholstery before we'd even reached the edge of Austin's city limits.

Then after a gentle nudge, a prod and a sharp poke, followed by the thrum of Zeke's sexy voice in my ear, awareness returned. I felt like a sloth in need of an extended vacation.

"The neighbors might get suspicious if I have to carry you into your apartment."

"I'm up," I mumbled and yawned.

The fantasy of awakening in bed beside a certain Ranger stunted as the passenger door interrupted my stretch.

Zeke chuckled. "Yeah right. Come on, princess. Looks like an early night for you."

Darkness had already descended over downtown Dallas as Zeke tugged my deadweight carcass from the truck cab and steadied me against him. The warm embrace kept the chill breeze at bay as I settled into the familiar nook beneath his arm.

Good time memories flooded through my brain as it slogged up from sleep stage to arousal. "What time is it?"

"Nearing nine," Zeke responded, holding the door open to my building. "We were waylaid by an accident on the interstate."

"Why's it so dark already?" I shivered. "And cold?"

"Storm's moving in."

I encircled his waist with my arms and snuggled up in the empty elevator to keep warm. The rickety old thing always gave me visions of death waiting to happen, but I suppose Zeke wasn't too keen on towing me up four flights of stairs.

The ancient elevator started with a jerk, throwing us into the corner and giving new meaning to the phrase *I'm up*. Then I noticed where my hand rested.

Stale beer breath varnished with *eau de morning mouth* didn't deter Zeke. Or me. Dreams of falling into bed and sleeping the night away vanished when his lips caught mine.

At the elevator's ding, he dragged me up the length of his body without breaking the kiss, and I wrapped my legs around his torso.

"Where's your keys?" Zeke asked around my lips, propping me against my apartment door.

I whipped my purse around to his spine, fished the jangle from the depths without opening my eyes, and crushed the keys into one of the hands cupping my butt.

I didn't want to think about what once was. I only wanted right now, which entailed Big Z in my bed doing all sorts of dirty deeds beneath my unmentionables. The thought alone made me groan.

But all thoughts of a night tangled together fled when Zeke dropped me on unsteady legs like a bag of bricks, shoved me behind him, and drew his weapon with an exclamation.

"What the hell?"

CHAPTER NINETEEN

To say a tornado had torn through my apartment would've been kind.

The truth? It appeared more as if someone had detonated a nuclear bomb.

Stuffing from the sofa and chair cushions blanketed the floor like snow. Dishes lay shattered across the kitchen and canned goods rolled along the tile. My happy hour supplies dripped down the open refrigerator door and into the now unfrozen foods while the rest was sopped up by the loaf of bread.

Whoever had laid waste to my apartment even went so far as to rip open my dining chair cushions and slaughter the glass-top table simply for sport.

My mother had given me that dining set, damnit!

Anger and outrage infused every pore of my being until fear diffused and drained it like cold water over pasta.

"My baby!"

Zeke grabbed my arm as I sought to sweep past him. "Stay put until I clear the apartment."

"But Slinky. All this glass. He could be hurt or…" My wail sputtered to a stop. I wouldn't even consider the possibility my sweet tabby cat might be gone.

"Stay here." The firm set of his jaw and intense stare brooked no opposition.

Weapon drawn, Zeke crept through the apartment, checking behind overturned furniture and the kitchen island, peering into closets and the bathroom before disappearing around the corner into the bedroom.

Seeing him in action offered a whole new perspective and gave me an even deeper appreciation for my Ranger.

I mean ex-boyfriend.

That guy I was about to surrender to.

Again.

Oh hell.

All the while, I watched and listened for any sign of my precious kitty. Slinky just had to be okay somewhere in this mess. I couldn't live without him. After all, he'd rescued and adopted me shortly after the epic breakup a few years ago.

Yep, that's what I said – *he* rescued *me*.

It was a dark and stormy night.

Yeah I know, cliché but in this case also very true.

I'd come home from the bar, still feeling the sting of betrayal, opened the single-car garage I paid extra for every month, and caught in my headlights what appeared to be a drowned rat slinking into the dry space. As I cautiously exited my Vette, the constant mewling revealed not a rat but a tiny kitten, sopping wet, cold and afraid.

Oh, and obviously quite hungry as he sucked on a fingertip like it was a sausage.

Feelings of betrayal and anger had melted by the time I finished drying him off in my apartment and gazed into big green eyes staring from fur fluffed out like a dandelion gone to seed.

The name? Since the night he'd slunk into my garage and spent the following weeks slinking around my apartment as if he expected danger around every corner, I thought Slinky appropriate.

Besides, you should see how high he springs in the air when he gets all riled up – er, when *I* get him all riled up.

Hey, a girl's gotta have some form of entertainment. Besides the adult variety, that is.

Zeke called out from the bedroom. "All clear, Vic, but you'd better get in here."

Nausea churned in my gut. I thought I was gonna hurl until I rounded the corner to my bedroom, saw Zeke standing with the door open to my walk-in closet, and heard the sweetest sound any mother could hear.

"Mero-o-o-w!"

"My baby!" I squealed and scooped Slinky into my arms. "How's momma's wittle baby kitty? Did wittle Slinky chase off those bad intruders? Yes, he did. Yes, he did."

When it comes to my cat, I'm a complete sucker. Or idiot. Really just an emotional basket case.

It wasn't until both our hearts stopped hammering and my kitty started purring that the scattered and tattered state of my bedroom came into focus.

Zeke broke the stunned silence as he flipped out his phone. "I guess you can retire *this* mattress."

Chaos descended on my apartment building for the second time in as many weeks.

The Dallas PD rifled through every nook and cranny, every drawer and dish, and left a fine layer of black fingerprint dust in their wake.

By the time they finished, you may as well have opened every door and window and just taken a hose to it all. Between the intruder and law enforcement, little remained salvageable.

Drool towel in tow, Jimmy-the-Super showed up to inspect the place, spoke briefly with the police, then made himself scarce without addressing me other than with a squinty-eyed stare.

I was surprised he'd even shown up at all, considering his probable gang and drug background. As soon as I cleaned up this disaster, I planned to send a scathing letter to the landlord to find out how pond scum qualified for a job that allowed access to honest citizens' homes.

When everything quieted down again, I took in the mess that was once my life. Nothing discernable remained of my furniture.

The tv and related electronics looked like victims of a drive-by shooting. My cast iron metal bedframe was intact, but without a mattress it was worthless for sleeping anytime in the near future. The wanton destruction left me in a quandary as midnight approached.

Going to Mom and Dad's was off the list. No way would I skulk to that place with my tail between my legs and witness firsthand the smug grin on the sperm donor's face.

Janine would let me hang out with her, but she still lived under the De'Laruse roof. News would travel from Mrs. De'Laruse's mouth to my parents' ears faster than the wind blows through West Texas.

Nick was out of town on some modeling gig last I knew, and Grady would probably let me stay with him, but that was just a bad idea all the way around.

A girl could handle only so much temptation – especially when vacillating between the aching need for comfort and the overwhelming desire to shoot someone's eyes out.

Or balls off.

If it weren't for the heat and the possibility of the cat having an accident, Slinky and I could spend the night in the garage curled up in my Vette. *Curled up* being the optimum word.

God love our military personnel, but I ain't one to fall asleep in a combat zone. Even though I was tired enough to fall out of my boots at that moment, I'm still too much of a pampered princess to sleep in those environs.

Zeke must've caught the sigh as I stared at the remains of my apartment. "If you can find anything in this mess, pack a bag. You'll sleep at my place tonight."

I narrowed my eyes. "We're standing among the wreckage of my life, and you're still trying to hook up with me?"

Zeke held up his hands in surrender. "Just sleep. Trust me, the urge has passed."

"Really?"

Should I be relieved or insulted?

"Getting involved with you again was a momentary lapse of my better judgment."

Definite insult.

But seeing as how no other offers were available at present, I should be grateful for a place to rest my head for the night.

Maybe.

I shoved the kitty carrier at Zeke and slogged through the bedroom debris to locate any clean clothes for the morrow. Then after picking my way across the glass-covered kitchen floor, I grabbed the litterbox and a couple tins of cat food and headed for our cars.

On the drive across town, a litany of questions tore through my beleaguered mind. Why me? Was this a random break-in? If so, it didn't appear they'd taken anything. Not that I had much of value.

Simply vandals searching for a good time? Were the perps looking for something in particular? If so, what? Money? Car keys? The thought of someone destroying my Vette made me see blood.

What if they'd hurt Slinky? That thought sent a shiver down my spine, and I patted the carrier for reassurance.

What if I'd been home? Yeah, that's where years of target practice would come in handy. My gun called to me.

My gun!

Most people raised in Texas learned how to shoot by the age of three and acquired their first weapon in their own name just as soon as they turned eighteen. My Sig Sauer P938 peashooter was good for smaller hands. Plus, it was a great way to pick up guys at the shooting range.

But I digress.

The moment I pulled into Zeke's apartment complex and parked beside his truck, I leapt out. "My gun!"

Zeke locked his truck and turned around to the passenger door of my car. "Relax. The police found it. It's in my waistband."

"Why'd they give it to you?"

"Good question, class. Why do you think?"

"It's registered. I've a carry permit."

Gathering up everything from the car and handing me Slinky's carrier, Zeke responded. "You were in no state to handle a weapon earlier."

"I want my gun," I demanded, following him into the building.

"You're in no state to handle a weapon now either."

"Give me my gun, Zeke Taylor."

"You might accidentally shoot that furball you're carrying." The elevator opened. "Do you really want that on your conscience right now?"

"Damnit, Zeke." I followed him in, the memory of the earlier elevator ride at my place springing to mind. "Just give me back my gun."

"Tomorrow."

"Now."

The sudden movement startled me as Zeke pressed in close, his breath warm.

Inviting. "Make me."

I set the carrier on the floor, pressed my body to his, then laid one on him that would scare a nun.

He jolted in surprise, dropped my bags and fisted my hair. As his tongue danced with mine, I wrapped my arms around him and trailed along his spine until I found what I wanted.

With a jerk and a shove, Zeke stumbled backward as I raised my arm in triumph, the Sig gleaming in my hand.

"Goes to show ya," I drawled. "Never come between a woman and her weapon."

CHAPTER TWENTY

The kitchen clatter woke me first. The moment Slinky noticed daylight hitting my retinas he let out a yowl to wake the dead.

Pretty much how I felt too.

Before falling asleep Slinky had spooned me. This morning he perched high atop my hip like he was the king of Mount Everest. Thank God he hadn't settled on my chest or he'd have thought he was king of the Himalayas.

You know, twin peaks?

Aw forget it.

"Do you have to make so much noise?" I called.

Zeke strolled over, wearing nothing but his royal blue boxers. He settled a mug on the coffee table.

"Rise and shine, princess."

I closed my eyes and groaned. "Need sleep. Not coffee."

"I offered you my bed, you know."

"Ain't happening with you in it too."

"Can't blame a guy for trying after that stunt you pulled last night."

My hand snaked out from the blanket and made contact with the mug. Coffee spread warmth through my innards as I gulped some down before opening my eyes a little wider this time.

"Don't you have a robe or something you can wear?"

Zeke shook his head. "Not like you haven't seen boxers before. Matter of fact, I think you bought these for me."

I squinted to focus. "Oh yeah." The wall clock grabbed my attention. If it wasn't for the fact I needed the cup of life-giving nectar, I'd have thrown the lot at him. "It's not even nine yet. Why'd you wake me so early on a Saturday?"

"I'm gonna run over to the office and get a little paperwork done."

"You country boys need to learn to sleep like us city girls once in awhile." I moaned, tugging the blanket over my face.

"Come on. I made a breakfast that might cheer you up."

Ham and eggs with hash browns sizzled as Zeke plopped the skillet on the table, the scent sending waves of encouragement that drove me from the sofa.

Ah, the cowboy's campfire breakfast, all stirred together as if we were on a cattle drive. Sometimes with crumbling bacon. Other times with sausage.

The familiar food was the only thing he'd made the countless times I'd slept over while we'd dated. Little ever changed where Zeke Taylor was concerned.

And there was a strange comfort in that.

"Thanks again for letting me stay last night," I said around a mouthful.

"Yer welcome." He got up to refill his coffee. "Have you considered the nature of the break-in?"

"I'm trying not to," I mumbled between bites.

"Was there anything valuable someone might want?"

"What could they want? They trashed the electronics. Most of the furniture was acquired from thrift stores. The only nice thing I had was the dining set Mom bought for me."

"I remember." Eyes sharpened. Lips thinned. Face blanked with no expression. Human Zeke disappeared into Ranger mode. "No other valuables then?"

"Besides my wardrobe and shoe collection?"

"There's the gun," Zeke muttered.

"Which they didn't take," I reminded him.

His upper lip twitched ever so slightly as if remembering my antics from last night. "The timing is interesting, you being out of town with me all day."

"Yeah. Normally I'd have been sleeping off the night before then cleaning around the apartment."

"Cleaning?"

I flashed him a dirty look as he took off for his bedroom, but he had me pegged. Saturdays were usually spent nursing a hangover. Maybe watching a little TV before trying to plan my outfit for the night.

Hey, I'm a girl. It takes a bit of time to look this good. Well, 'cept for at the moment. Felt like I'd been dragged behind a monster truck all the way from Austin.

"Anyway," I called after him. "As much as I want to categorize this as a random event, something about it feels off."

"The wanton destruction makes it personal."

That sent a chill down my spine. "I was afraid of that."

"So someone breaks into your apartment on a day you just so happen to alter your routine and leave town. They don't take anything, but toss your apartment anyway."

"Thanks for the recap to my pain."

Zeke strolled in all gussied up in dark jeans and buttoning a maroon shirt with his shoulder holster swinging from his arm and his Stetson firmly in place. He walked over the chairback and returned to sit at the table.

I used to think it was so hot when he did that – until it got old. I think he did it just to show off his manly stature and long legs. You know, because he could.

"Who all knew you were going to Austin with me?" Zeke asked.

While feeding a crumb of ham to Slinky, I contemplated the possibilities. "Well there's Grady, of course. Oh, and Radioman."

"Radioman?"

"The guy sitting at the bar last night when you came in." Slinky accepted a nibble of hash browns then licked the butter from my fingers with his rough tongue.

"The one in the middle of asking you for a date?"

"Which you so rudely interrupted."

"You might thank me for that one day."

"Don't flatter yourself."

"Anyone else?" he asked, adjusting the holster straps.

I thought for a second. "Maybe whoever Grady called in to work my shift, which now that I have to replace most of my furniture I really could've used."

"That's what insurance is for. No rush."

"Says the man in the black hat."

He inserted his service weapon into the holster with a shluck and a snap. "What about the super?

"Jimmy?"

The interaction we'd shared a few days ago reasserted in my addled brain. The winking skull tattoo. Jimmy staring down his nose when I'd questioned him about the unlocked rooftop access door. Yelling at me for his burnt steak.

Telling me all about my comings and goings – and with who.

Can you say suspect *numero uno*?

After the fuss I'd created the other morning, this visit was risky.

Dumber than my dad on a Saturday night. Denser than Janine when it came down to what to do with a guy trapped between the sheets. Ditzier than – well, me when I'd had one too many.

But if I was gonna get Bobby's carcass out of jail and do everything to prove his innocence, it was time to wave the white flag.

"Don't handle break-ins."

Detective Duncan's voice carried across the precinct when I walked into the room and made a beeline for his desk. Chatter and chuckles followed me, along with a few wolf whistles, which, given the state of my get-up and the bags under my eyes hanging down to my chin, made me wonder just how hard up some of the local yokels were.

Particularly the ones with glinting wedding bands.

So you've heard the one about how marriage kills the sex drive? I'm pretty sure my parents fit that particular state as well, though in their case it may have more to do with my dad's *roaming* sex drive than lack thereof.

Given his penchant for panty piñata, is it any wonder why I'm a bit jaded about the idea of marital bliss?

I plunked down on the corner of Duncan's desk. "How goes the serving and protecting thing, detective?"

He didn't even lift his waxy cue ball from the computer screen. "Here to turn yourself in?"

"For what?"

"How about detonating a nuclear bomb within the Dallas city limits?"

I crossed my long legs. "So you've heard about my apartment, huh?"

"Talk of the precinct this morning, sweetheart."

Don't you hate it when someone takes what's supposed to be a term of endearment and turns it into something derisive?

Me too. Kinda reminded me of eating snails – slimy and a bit tough to swallow.

"Wondered if I could talk to you about it, since Zeke introduced us and all."

That earned me an irreverent snort. "Most people wouldn't call that an introduction."

"Seeing as you used my one phone call to contact him instead of throwing me in jail, I'd say it could be construed as such."

Duncan shook his head and continued abusing the keyboard, pecking the keys like a woodpecker after a worm. "This is homicide, sweetheart. You need to go one floor down for breaking and entering."

"More like assault and battery," I mumbled.

The pecking stopped while wide eyes gave me the once over. "I thought you weren't home."

"I wasn't," I reassured. "But the wanton destruction makes this personal. Like an assault on my person."

An eye roll was all I got for my efforts. "Like I said, one floor down."

"So why were you threatening me with breaking and entering the other night if all you do is homicide?"

"Because you were breaking and entering on my homicide case," Duncan retorted. "Which, by the way, I could still charge you for."

Okay, new tactic. "Zeke thinks what happened last night with my apartment, your case, and something he's working on might be connected."

"And Ranger Taylor couldn't be bothered to come downtown himself? He had to send his little lusty liaison who thinks she's the next Nancy Drew?"

"Am not!"

"Tell me something I don't already know."

What was it with all the Nancy Drew references? First Zeke and now Detective Duncan. I thought only girls read those books while boys gravitated toward the Hardy Boys.

My high pitch garnered a few head turns. I lowered my voice. "Okay, fine. But you saw the certain Mexican official's name tied to Amy Vernet, yes?"

"I did."

"Well, on my jaunt with Zeke to the capitol, I discovered said official is officially, yet technically unofficially, Amy's father."

Now I had the detective's attention. "So Juarez really is her father?"

I nodded.

Duncan's brow furrowed deeper than a prairie dog's hole. "But what do you mean by officially yet unofficially?"

I smiled. Asking me questions? Now he was intrigued – which meant I had the detective right where I wanted him.

"The original record, which according to Madam Bitchy in vital statistics is no longer the original somehow, was changed to remove his name for reasons unknown. Now the amended is classified as the original, though I still don't get how the original is no longer considered the original."

"Odd."

"I thought so too."

Duncan pondered the implications with a swipe of sweat from his knob. "Removing a name from a birth record would require a court order."

"Which someone got."

With a flourish befitting a matador, I pulled from my purse yesterday's acquired envelope – from what turned out to be a very expensive day – and plopped it onto Duncan's desk. He stared me up and down with almost, dare I say, respect.

I did say *almost*, right?

"Does Zeke keep you around for all his legwork?" Duncan asked with a smirk at my enticing extremities.

The obvious double-entendre deserved a scathing comeback. Maybe something about men and their unhealthy attachment to their third leg.

That is until my mind about gave me whiplash when it reminded me of last night's elevator lip lock. And the wall press.

Though I'd put a screeching halt to the tangled two-step with Zeke, I was definitely way overdue for some legwork. When did Nick say he'd be home?

Then again, Radioman was in town, available and obviously willing.

Focus, Vicki!

"Zeke took me along because he can't be tied to Amy's case, even though we both have a strong personal interest in Bobby's innocence."

"And that right there is why both of you need to stay out of it and leave this case to me."

"W-What? Why?"

"You're both personally vested in and committed to Vernet's innocence," Duncan returned.

"But he *is* innocent."

"Personal feelings cloud the facts, sweetheart."

And I thought we'd made real progress after the events of the other night. Well, forget that. Duncan just landed right back on my bad vibe list.

"Then I'll just have to find Amy's killer on my own."

"Go home, Nancy Drew, and leave the investigating to the professionals."

The detective opened a desk drawer and made to file away Amy's birth records. The records I'd suffered so much humiliation to get. Records that cost me more of my hard-earned money. Documents that left me with little sleep the past three days and had left my apartment all shattered and tattered.

Oh hell-to-the-no with a capital H.

In one fluid movement, I snatched the envelope from Duncan's hand, leapt from the desk, and sauntered across the precinct as fast as my getaway sticks would carry me.

"Hey, bring that back here, sweetheart."

"Make me."

"I can have you arrested for absconding with information in an official police investigation."

"I never said I'd give it to you," I said, pressing the elevator button. "Besides, I paid for this and have a receipt to prove it."

"I'll get a court order!" Duncan yelled.

"Go ahead. Then take it down to Austin like I did. I'll even give you the name of the lady to see in vital statistics."

Yeah right. *Lady* was a definite stretch for Madam Bitchy.

CHAPTER TWENTY-ONE

"Where do you want these?"

Janine held up a couple of books that appeared to have escaped my apartment's bombing. I stopped sweeping glass long enough to wipe the sweat from my eyes and focus attention away from the mess.

The never-ending mess.

I sighed. "Put 'em in the bedroom closet with what's left of my clothes."

As Janine scuttled away to do my bidding, I sank into the window seat and took stock. After two hours of sorting, shoveling, sweeping, and stowing we'd only made a miniscule dent in the debris field.

Between the two of us, we'd spent the first thirty minutes simply trying to decide where to begin and the next thirty minutes picking through my strewn-about wardrobe and hanging what we could in the closet for later inspection.

Since the damage in there was minimal, we'd dubbed it the 'safe zone' a place to put anything deemed worthy of keeping. What it contained was achingly miniscule compared to what it had held BB – Before Bombing.

If it wasn't shredded it was embedded with glass particles and debris no amount of washing or dry cleaning would ever make wearable again.

By the ninety minute mark, we'd succeeded in carving out pathways connecting the rooms so walking wasn't so hazardous, and discovered a package of precious Oreos ground like dust into the carpet. That made me hotter than a menopausal middle-aged woman, until Janine offered to donate a package to the *Victuals for Vicki* fund.

Then we moved the destroyed mattress against the wall near the apartment entry, discovered the box springs untouched – hallelujah – and returned a few unbroken dresser drawers to their rightful home.

With some nails, industrial-strength hot glue, a lot of prayer – from Janine – and more than a few curse words tossed into the ether – from me – a couple of additional drawers had the potential for useful status again.

Yeah…no.

The bottom of the second hour had us in the bathroom desperately sweeping up glass from the shattered mirror, vanity light globes, and the old sliding glass shower doors.

Hey, a girl can only hold it so long before nature stops calling and pounds her fist on the bladder, screaming at the top of her lungs.

And yes, nature is always referred to in the feminine. Ever hear of Mother Nature?

I rest my case.

After going over and over the tiled floor with a broom and dustpan, and getting little but the larger chunks, Janine stepped in with the super-sized shop vac and sucked up those microscopic shards faster than a tornado on a Tuesday.

With the glassed-in shower doors gone, maybe Jimmy-the-Super would remove the tacky brass framing so I could install a tension rod and curtain.

Jimmy. Humph.

I wasn't sure I wanted that man in my apartment, considering he was suspect one on my list of destructors. No sign of forced entry meant someone was either a really good lock picker or they entered with a key.

Maybe that someone was also responsible for accessing the rooftop door and throwing Amy into the parking lot below. All the red blinking neon signs pointed to my super.

Guess what I would be buying and installing on my door as an early birthday present?

The only thing that didn't make sense was what Jimmy gained by killing Amy. With the tattoos covering an assortment of muscle big enough to pulverize a tank – or an apartment – the *how* wasn't even an issue.

Perhaps he was simply the muscle in a drug gang war and ordered to kill her. Made sense to me. But then who was pulling Jimmy's strings?

A muffled knock at my front door. No way!

Please don't let it be Jimmy. Please don't let it be Jimmy.

A peek through the peep hole sent my fear into overdrive. I unlocked the door then inched it open, hoping to avoid the worst.

"Uh...hi, Mom."

The scent of nail polish hovered around her. Fresh hair color and blunt ends swung from a new cut. Yep, Mom had been at the salon, which meant she'd probably just dropped off *her* best friend after a day of beauty.

Which meant only one thing.

"Hello, dear. I was just talking with Mrs. De'Laruse and...good heavens!" Mom pressed the door open and pushed past me. "What in God's good name have you done to your apartment, Victoria?"

Janine came racing into the living room all bug-eyed and looking like she'd just been bushwhacked. My best friend had obviously broken our cardinal rule and told her mother where she was headed. Then her mother had then talked to my mother.

Word between our families spreads like a wildfire during a West Texas drought. I offered Janine my best stare down before readdressing my mother.

"Just doing a little spring cleaning, Mom. Care to join us?"

"It's summer," Mom deadpanned, staring at the mounds of stuffing that had once padded my couch and chairs.

"Way to state the obvious," I muttered.

"Was this why you left in such a rush?" Mom directed to Janine.

Janine blanched. "Well I...um...didn't want..."

Since the time our mothers did diaper duty, my best friend never could handle being put on the spot. 'Specially when cornered by either her mother or mine.

When we were teens and had stayed out late or snuck into a party where we weren't allowed – for which I take full blame – all my mom had to do was give Janine the *look*. Poor girl would practically pee her pants and spill faster than water down a waterslide.

For years I'd tried to teach her a good poker face – alas, to no avail. Instead she just seemed constipated.

"Relax, Mom," I intervened. "My apartment was broken into last night, is all."

"How can you say *relax* and *break-in* all in the same sentence?" Her eyes widened when she took in the wreck that used to be the dining table she'd bought. "Your lovely dinette. The chairs!"

You know that saying about never coming between a momma bear and her cub? When my mom's green eyes glinted and flashed like lightning before a hailstorm, I understood it right quick.

You ever see a momma bear in action when her cub has been threatened? Made *me* about pee my pants – and I'm the cub in this particular drama.

Mom whipped out her cell phone faster than the credit card on a shopping spree.

"Reginald? We have a problem."

Next to Mrs De'Laruse, Reginald von Braun was my mother's dearest friend.

'Course that might have more to do with the fact my mother provides ample support of his interior decorating business too.

For as long as I can remember, every three years he completely overhauled my parents' home. Not to mention the annual rounds of Easter, Independence Day, fall – we didn't dare call it Halloween – and Christmas décor with accompanying soirees. The only thing he was never allowed to touch was the Christmas tree, as Mom liked to save that bit of decorating as a family tradition.

She may as well have let him participate there too. With Reginald on speed dial and at the house for one reason or another, it was safe to say he was as close to family as I'd ever known.

Hell, I liked him better than my own father.

So it was perfectly reasonable to tear up a bit when Reginald's dark, round face peeked around my door before throwing it wide open with his usual panache.

"Victoria, *mein liebchen!*" Reginald cried as he wrapped his gangly arms around my waist and buried my face in his hairy chest, before kissing both cheeks then holding me at arm's length. "Naughty, naughty, naughty to leave Reginald for so long."

"It's good to see you, Reggie," I replied, taking in the peach and hot pink flamenco shirt ruffles fluttering with his boundless energy.

Only Reggie could make that combination work.

I'm also the only person in the Dallas/Fort Worth metroplex capable of getting away with shortening his name. It might have a little to do with the fact it was easier for a two-year-old to say.

But as I got older and wiser, it grew clear the German accent was fake. Which meant the name was likely fake.

It might also have something to do with Zeke's discovery that Reginald's real name was Reggie Brown. And he had a juvie record. All of which I kept mum from my mom.

Still, Reggie was living proof that with enough hard work, dedication, and talent – not to mention the right connections – anyone could rehab their image from bad boy to the area's leading interior designer. Texas mojo and the American entrepreneurial spirit at its finest.

Just don't judge him by the personal fashion sense.

Reggie looked wide-eyed at my living room, pursed his lips then chucked my chin. "So zis is where leettle Victoria has been hiding herself, no?"

Mom interjected, "Some thief had the audacity to break into my daughter's apartment. Just look at the place."

After a quick peck in greeting to both Mom and Janine, Reggie took my mother's advice. No one spoke as Reggie followed the cat trails we'd created through the heap that had become my apartment.

A *hmm* vibrated from the bedroom. *Tsk-tsk* echoed in the bathroom before he made his return to the living room.

With one hand on his black leather-clad hip and the other with a finger at the corner of his lips, Reggie completed a series of three-hundred-and-sixty degree turns encompassing the living, dining, and kitchen before passing sentence.

"Zis place is a mess."

I laughed out loud at the obvious.

"But not beyond saving, *mein liebchen*," Reggie continued with a flourish of his hands. "Zis is why mothers call Reginald, no?"

"Where do you think we should start?" Mom asked.

"Don't you think we should finish cleaning first?" Janine put in.

I simply stood by and watched the show, knowing I'd lost complete control of my apartment the moment Mom hit speed dial. But even in the loud outfit, I trusted Reginald.

I think.

Maybe.

"Not to worry," Reggie said, "tis all part of zee plan." A sharp clap of his hands made all of us jump. "Han!"

Reggie's diminutive Asian assistant came scurrying in, pushing a small, metal cart loaded with decorator books, fabric swatches, carpet swatches, paint and tile samples, you name it. I immediately felt a headache coming on and wanted to hug the medicine cabinet like an accountant during tax season.

Only the medicine cabinet was no longer there.

"Um, Mom?" I called, joining her overlooking the kitchen island. "Not that I don't appreciate seeing Reggie, but I can no longer afford to piddle in your park. How much is this gonna cost me?"

"That reminds me," Mom said. "Reginald, this place needs a full and total remodel. Design, furniture, electronics, everything. Include a full security system as well."

Reggie's ebony eyes shined with dollar signs. Han sped up laying out sample books across the counter.

I felt like I'd just been bucked from a bronco into next week.

"I can't afford this, Mom."

"Really, Victoria. Who do you think is paying for it all?"

The black AmEx came to mind. I considered my words carefully. "Dad?"

"Exactly," she replied without missing a beat. "Since it's obvious you won't be returning to the family home anytime soon, I need the assurance that my daughter is comfortable and safe. What's a few hundred thousand to a mother's peace of mind?"

It's not a piddle in the park, that's for sure.

CHAPTER TWENTY-TWO

With a need to wash my tainted clothes, not to mention desperation to escape the madness overtaking my apartment, I snatched up a load or two in a basket and crept downstairs to the communal laundry.

I had to have something to wear to work tonight.

Normally on Saturdays I wore something awesome and sexy. Made me feel all flirty, which helped me connect with patrons of the male persuasion, which garnered better tips.

However, most of those little numbers were dry clean only types. Even though my mother would offer to pay for the one-hour dry cleaning service, the remodel of my apartment was more than enough to set her back for a bit.

I just didn't want to milk it any more than necessary. After all, I was a proud independent woman now.

Mostly.

After dumping denim in one washer and colors in another, I sat down in a corner and fought the urge to fall asleep. Forty minutes later, the buzz woke me enough to stumble across the room to fill a dryer before reentering dreamland and all it entailed.

LOOK BEFORE YOU JUMP

Made me miss Nick even more. Maybe he'd returned from parts unknown and we could meet up at the bar tonight for a session of extreme stress release. It'd save me having to face Zeke again.

Until I had to pick up Slinky in the morning.

I couldn't keep treating my poor, traumatized kitty to a life of vagrancy, staying at Zeke's one night and somewhere else the next. If I could just get my apartment cleaned up and buy a new mattress, I could stay here. Honest I could.

'Cause even though he'd probably say yes, asking Nick to let us shack up with him for a few days was too intimate. Out of the question.

No way, no how, and a great big *hell* no.

The snort and drool trickle woke me from my musings right before the dryer buzzed. A few other tenants had arrived for laundry duty, so I shoved mine into the basket and lugged my exhausted and stiff carcass up to the fourth floor.

It's amazing what big, strong men can accomplish in less than two hours. And I ain't talking between the sheets.

In my absence, Reggie had called in the cavalry – and then some. About ten sweaty guys swarmed my one-bedroom apartment, tugging up carpet, ripping cabinets from my kitchen, and carrying out the final remnants of the trash heap.

My jaw almost hit the floor at the nearly blank slate.

"What in the h...heck?"

I quickly modified my preferred wording when Mom turned around from where she stood by the window seat, ear to the phone and jaw determined. Thankfully Slinky's favorite window seat haunt hadn't been destroyed.

Yet.

Jimmy-the-Super stood in the center of my living room, alternately yelling at the workers to stop tearing up carpet and targeting Reggie and Han, who pretty much ignored him and continued comparing swatches and paint samples.

Janine was nowhere to be found.

Then the bedroom door crept open a fraction of an inch and a recognizable blue eye shown through the crack. I scuttled past everyone and joined her before dropping the laundry basket on the vacant floor of my bedroom.

"What's going on, Janine?"

"Your mom's gone a little, shall we say, nuts."

"I can see that."

"She and Reginald got it in their heads to do a complete overhaul of your apartment," Janine replied, "including structural."

So much for buying a new mattress and staying here during a quick reno. "But she can't do that. I don't own, I rent."

"Which is why your super is here raising cain. He's threatened to call the cops."

"Oh great, just what I need right now. More vice visitors."

Janine's cell phone rang. While she spoke to her mom, I contemplated what it would be like to watch the police haul my bound and determined mother off to jail.

I doubted if I could convince them to trade her out for my dad instead. After all, his AmEx card was the culprit behind this current chaos.

When Janine hung up her phone, my brain shifted gears with her words faster than my Vette on the freeway.

"Bobby's been bailed from jail."

The yellow crime scene barrier was gone when we pulled up to Bobby's house.

Freshly showered, shaved, and shirted, he answered the door with a surprising sparkle in his blue eyes.

"I've found my new mission," Bobby said before Janine or I could ask.

We followed him into the living room in stunned silence and sat together on the beige couch while he continued the stunning reveal.

"I'm gonna start a prison ministry."

Janine was the first to find her tongue. "But what about the children's pastorate at the church?"

"Dad's already begun the search for someone else to fill that position."

"Wait a minute," I said with just a touch of heat. "Your father *fired* you?"

"No, no, no," Bobby reassured. "I quit."

Janine's big eyes grew wider. "But why?"

Lurching to his feet, Bobby began the familiar pacing of a caged tiger. 'Cept this time he seemed more energized and excited than apathetic or pissed-off.

"Don't you see? God always brings something good out of the bad."

Janine and I just stared at each other.

"Still not following you," I said.

Bobby stopped, his animated hand movements reminding me of his dad's once Pastor Dennis got wound up during a Sunday sermon.

"I couldn't go back and serve in children's ministry. Not after…you know," Bobby admitted with a bob of his Adam's apple.

Janine dabbed at her eyes. Uh-oh.

Danger! Danger! Snot bubble developing at two o'clock.

"But after a deep and personal inside look at the souls languishing in prison, experiencing the fear and dejection firsthand, one night while in my bunk God thumped me on the head with a new vision."

Maybe God had thumped Bobby a little too hard.

"Aren't prison ministries a dime a dozen?" I asked.

"Yes," Bobby acknowledged. "But most are simply to offer up a sermon here and a word there. Those shepherds have no idea what it's really like eating, sleeping, and trying to mentally survive minute-by-minute in such an environment. They don't know how to truly reach the heart and soul of a prisoner."

"And after four nights behind bars, you do?" I challenged.

"It may as well have been four years. In those four days, I learned more about myself than I'd thought possible. About what Paul and the disciples experienced during the early days of the church. Made more of an impact than any sermon, I tell you. This is it…I know it. It's what Amy would've wanted."

"That's powerful," Janine said, her voice tinged with awe.

Their blue-eyed gazes locked in spiritual wonder.

I just rolled mine. "I hate to be the bad news bearer, but this ministry is a moot cause if the charges aren't dropped or you aren't proven innocent of Amy's death."

That sat Bobby down. "Have you discovered anything new?"

I nodded. "Zeke thinks there's some sort of connection between Amy's death and a case he's working. I spent all day yesterday with him down in Austin checking out Amy's birth records." I pulled the envelope from my purse and handed it to him. "You were right about Amy's father."

"What about Amy's father?" Janine asked.

"It's probably best you don't know," I replied.

With arms crossed over her chest, Janine plopped against the couch arm, offering me her best irritated drama queen stare. Papers scattered across the other couch arm as Bobby dug through the pile until discovering the golden ticket.

I knew immediately when he saw the name.

"Jackpot," he muttered. "I was right. It's connected to the cartel."

"What cartel?" Janine asked, interest piqued again.

Someday she'd thank me for keeping her in the dark.

Late afternoon and I had about two hours until I had to be at the bar.

That gave me enough time to drop Janine at her car, thank her profusely for giving up her Saturday, then sneak past the super and up the stairs to the room that used to be my apartment.

At least the empty shell no longer looked like a tornado had passed through, save for the fine particles clouding the air like high humidity in spring. But I still wondered where I'd sleep that night. Or tomorrow night.

The next few weeks anyone?

Mom was still in full sergeant mode, so arguing was as pointless as breathing underwater.

I simply grabbed the basket of clean laundry, gave her a kiss, and handed over the apartment key with instructions to let me know when I could return. Then I hightailed it across town to the Ranger Residence Inn to beg for mercy.

Zeke greeted me with a bare chest, bare feet hanging below his lounge pants, and a half-eaten piece of meat works pizza in his hand. The grumble of my stomach protested another skipped meal.

My nether regions? Yeah, they were protesting a skipped something too.

Think about it.

"Early dinner?" I asked.

"Late lunch," Zeke said and took a bite. "Come to rescue your cat?" He glanced down at the laundry basket at my hip. "Guess not."

"I, uh...might need to impose on your hospitality a little longer."

The door swung open wider and Zeke padded into the living room without offering to carry my burden like a chivalrous knight.

"I get paid time-and-a-half for cat sitting on weekends," he called over his shoulder.

So much for chivalry.

"I'll remember that."

Reentering the devil's lair, I dropped the basket with a smack on the foyer tiles before joining Zeke at the couch and finding Slinky reclining next to him watching the Texas Rangers whip on the Astros.

When Zeke offered up a sliver of ham, I knew my fickle feline had flipped to the opposing side faster than a free-agent in the offseason.

I narrowed my eyes at the furball. "Traitor."

"I take it the clean-up at *Chateau d' Vicki* remains ongoing?"

I hesitated. "You could say that."

Zeke arched his brow. "I take it there's more?"

"More? No. Try less."

"I don't follow."

I sighed and plopped down on the couch with the cat ensconced between us.

Safety in numbers, you know.

As if expecting me, there was already a second empty plate and bottle of beer with a condensation puddle on my side of the pizza box. A greedy pull went a long way toward quenching my thirst.

"Janine told her mother," I started. "Who in turn told my mother. Who then showed up at my apartment."

Zeke nodded. "Ah, the church ladies food chain."

"Mom got one look at the place and went into momma bear mode so fast, this cub had to run for her life."

That got me a chuckle. "So how does that constitute less instead of more?"

"Mom called Reggie, and his team cleared out the place. I'm talking cleared out and cleaned up as if I'd never lived there. Someone else could move in at this point…well, if there were any kitchen cabinets left."

"A free makeover courtesy of your mom," Zeke said. "That's cool."

"No, it's not," I whined. "No food. No furniture. Not even a mattress to sleep on. I've become a homeless vagrant."

"You're not homeless. You and the cat can stay here as long as you need." Another piece of ham disappeared into Slinky's mouth. "I'll even let you sleep on my mattress tonight."

"Oh huh-uh. I'll have to find some other way to pay you back."

"Relax," Zeke said as he got up and took his plate to the kitchen. "I'll be gone. You'll have the whole place to yourself tonight."

The retort died on my lips. Did Ranger Boy have a girlfriend? If so, he'd failed to mention it when he'd hog-tied me into the little recon trip to Austin. Then there were the kisses in the elevator and the clenching in my hallway.

'Course I already knew Zeke was the two-timing type. But I'd never imagined being the two-time'er instead of the two-time'ee.

Or was that the other way around?

I lurched to my feet. "Does she know I stayed here last night?"

"What? Who?"

"Your girlfriend!"

"Gee Vic," he said. "Do you really think I'd...?"

"You've done it before," I accused.

Full lips thinned into a firm line. Eyes hardened into dark orbs.

"If you must know, I'm conducting a stake-out tonight. Now if you'll excuse me, I need to get a few hours of sleep."

In three strides, he walked past the couch and toward the bedroom.

"Zeke, I didn't mean..."

"The spare key is on the kitchen counter. I'll see you tomorrow." With that, Zeke slammed the bedroom door shut.

Sometimes I wished I could do the same thing to my lips. You know, before I said stupid things. Put my foot in my mouth.

Damn disease.

CHAPTER TWENTY-THREE

Saturday evening traffic moved along at a satisfying clip.

One thing I loved about Texas was that the speed limit was more a suggestion than an actual ticketable offense. Out-of-towners were more likely to get a fine for going below the *minimum* posted speed limit.

That's right. Around these here parts, you better make sure you've got enough hitch in your giddyup, or you'll pay for going too slow. 'Cept during rush hour.

You remember. That misnomer I mentioned?

After getting the evil eye from Zeke, I'd wanted nothing more than to get ready for work and skedaddle out of there. The more I thought about our exchange, the more I realized how much my words had hurt the guy.

I mean, he had devastated me once before by two-timing me, but that was more than two years ago. Now I went and accused him of using me as a cheatable offense on a non-existent girlfriend.

It was obvious I hadn't forgiven Zeke. I was holding onto the past like a druggie to his pipe and needles just waiting for the next fix.

Maybe he had changed. Learned from the mistakes he'd made with me. If Bobby and Amy could let go of their pasts, why couldn't I?

The thought of Amy's death sent me into deep thought. Because of my big mouth, the police had reopened the case and reclassified it as a murder instead of a suicide.

Because of my big mouth, they thought Bobby responsible for his wife's death.

Because of my big mouth, Zeke had dragged me to Austin to discover connections between Amy and a known cartel.

What did all of these events have in common?

Besides my big mouth.

I only had an inkling of a clue. But Zeke obviously saw the bigger picture. Something involving tonight's stakeout.

If I was going to help Bobby and find out who had killed Amy, I needed inside information only Zeke could provide. And if the tight-lipped Ranger Taylor wasn't gonna cooperate, there was only one thing left for me to do.

Horns honked, tires squealed, and rubber burned as I slung the Vette across three lanes of traffic to exit before turning around to head back in the direction I'd come.

Like Bobby, I had a new mission.

With the entire gang on tap every Saturday night, I had the delusion I might get away from the bar ahead of schedule.

That theory went out the window about the time Bud disappeared a good half hour before closing. About the same time when the night's hookups made their escape and the crowd thinned.

My mood had soured before then anyway.

Since the remainder of the evening's activities dictated sobriety, I'd held my libations to one measly beer all night.

Count 'em – one.

A non-inebriated Vicki made for a boring and cranky Vicki. The music was dull. The customers uninteresting. Conversations with my co-workers stilted. Even Grady's advancements left me cold.

Was this what I had to look forward to if I laid off the getting laid?

Please, oh please don't answer that.

While old Wanker offered the final call and Rochelle and Baby gathered glasses, Grady sidled up and pressed in behind me with a nip at my ear.

"Something on your mind, Vic?"

Warm breath didn't trigger the usual response in my nether regions as I continued rinsing out a tray of dirty beer glasses and loading them in the dishwasher.

"Just the usual."

"Ah," Grady replied. "Bud leaving early."

"No," I said behind gritted teeth, letting my exasperation show.

"Headache?"

"No."

"Stomachache?"

"No."

"That time of the month?"

My elbow to his ribs and a face-full of suds made Grady release me with a spit and a chuckle.

"None of your business, but hell no."

He turned me around to face him, dark eyes growing serious. "I've noticed that Nick guy hasn't been around this week. Did y'all have a fight or somethin'?"

"He's been out of town."

A tilt of the mustache. "I'm available."

I flipped a towel at him with a snap. "Thanks, but I don't need any further complications right now."

"Roll reversal time then. The patron usually spills to the bartender, so maybe the bartender needs to spill to the patron this time."

"But you're not a patron. You're the proprietor."

"They both start with *p*, Miss Smart-Ass." Grady turned around and leaned against the nearby counter for a more direct view – and not of my assets this time. "So tell me what's on your mind. Does this have something to do with a certain Ranger?"

"A little." I paused, unsure how much I should reveal. Aw, screw it. "We've got a mutual friend who's been in some trouble. Accused of killing his wife."

"Is this about that pastor in the news?"

So much for worrying about a great big and mysterious reveal.

I nodded. "Zeke played basketball with him in high school, and Bobby and I...let's just say we have a long history."

"Long history as in..."

"As in firmly lodged in the past where it belongs," I barked.

That got me a smirk that raised his brows. Too bad it didn't get me a raise in pay though. I really could've used the extra cash at the moment.

"So this isn't about hookin' up with Zeke again?"

"No! Where did you get such an idea?"

Grady shrugged. "I assumed something was percolating between y'all again when he asked ya to go to Austin."

"Believe me. There's nothing percolating between us."

Besides the elevator moment. And the hallway. Last night?

"What was the trip for then?" Grady asked.

"Zeke thinks there's a tie between Bobby's wife's death and a case he's working on."

"And he needed *your* help?"

I could take offense to that little emphasis but decided to let it go and move on.

If only I could do the same with the ex. "Rangers investigate only within their mandate, unless there's a link to an outside case."

"So how does her death tie to his case?"

"Can't answer that," I responded.

"What is his case?" the boss man asked.

"Can't answer that either."

"Can't or won't?"

"I plead the fifth?"

Very mysterious. Very Bond'esque. Let the man wonder, even though *I* still wasn't exactly sure what Zeke's case was all about. But considering the Juarez name connected a Mexican cartel to Amy, it didn't take more than a high school diploma to determine it pertained to drugs.

This *is* Texas, you know.

I got the onceover before Grady pronounced sentence on me. "You gonna be okay to drive tonight?"

Not quite the sentence I was expecting, but seeing as I had work to do after I got off work, I'd take it. "I'm more than okay. I limited myself to one beer tonight."

"All that religious association having an effect on ya, Vic?"

"Nah. Just feeling the need not to tempt the statistic gods tonight."

Grady set his jaw and straightened his shoulders. "Still...you be careful goin' home, ya hear?"

A shiver passed up my spine at the serious glint in his eyes before my boss walked away. It was almost as if something from his long ago military days had returned to threaten him.

I shook off the weird vibe, finished cleaning up, then walked with the staff to our cars. Only Grady remained behind in his office. At the bar.

Alone.

After pulling into a well-lit, twenty-four-hour convenience store parking lot, I dragged my earlier new purchase from underneath the passenger seat. The laptop powered up and glowed in the darkened interior of my car.

One benefit of carrying the Bohanan name? It was pretty well-known in elite stores around the area – even among the tech crowd.

Mom had accounts set up across the metroplex, where acceptable members of the household staff could pick up things for the family and have a bill forwarded at the end of the month. The approved list rarely changed, my mom much more loyal to her staff than the elder Vernets were with theirs.

I'd taken a real chance in assuming my parents hadn't removed my name from said list after moving out. But the freckle-faced manager recognized me and didn't even bother checking to see if I was still *acceptable* in the company's eyes.

One bullet dodged.

Hey, I needed a new computer anyway after mine had been thrashed and trashed during the break-in. No need to wait for my mom to buy the inevitable.

The manager had even loaded the tracking software and given me a brief tutorial. I only hoped the device on Zeke's truck hadn't fallen off on a back road somewhere. Or that he'd gone out of range.

The program opened and a red dot blinked in rapid succession. Stationary, which told me Zeke was onsite at his stakeout.

The distance from town said I'd better fill up before leaving the c-store parking lot. That is, if I didn't want Zeke to have to rescue a stranded damsel in distress later. It'd be best if I could just hide out and watch him watching – supervise him watching?

Oh, whatever.

As long as I hightailed my carcass back to his apartment once I was done watching, Zeke could continue to delude himself into thinking I was unconcerned and unaware of the details of his case.

I'd dodge bullet number two that way.

Along the highway I made good time. Once on a side road, I had to slow down a bit to avoid the occasional roadkill or pothole. But my poor baby car was not prepared for rutted and washed-out dirt roads.

Dust swirled in my wake. Rocks pinged the paint job. The undercarriage intermittently dragged. I cringed every time like Janine used to do when a singer would screech a high note in church or be slightly off-key.

Personally, I never could tell the difference. Guess you had to be a true musician to hear it. And be bothered by it.

But I digress.

If not for the tracking device, I'd have missed the barely discernable turnoff. Trees and brush choked what looked like little more than an old cattle trail.

After skidding to a stop, I backed up and pulled my baby in close to the trees behind Zeke's truck and another vehicle, trying not to add any scratches to my already suffering exterior. The nails-on-the-chalkboard screech told me I hadn't succeeded.

Crickets chirped as I snuck down the trail, keeping close to the trees until walking through the remnants of Charlotte's web. In panty-piddling fear, I lurched from the trees, tripped on a rock, and tumbled into a dust and leaf-encrusted rut before grabbing my twisted ankle.

But I didn't cry out, mind you. My lips remained firmly pressed together, with a metallic tang on my tongue.

As I furiously brushed off hair and clothes, I could only hope the web had been unoccupied when I'd crashed the party.

A strap on my sandal had broken in my headlong fall. Scratches on my legs and my arms burned and itched. Or was that a spider bite?

Great. Just great. Why hadn't I thought to wear more appropriate gear for this stakeout? Probably because this city gal hadn't realized stakeouts were in the countryside too.

Talk about your equal opportunity.

As I stamped and slid my way along the trail like Frankenstein's hunchbacked assistant, darkness closed in around me. Clouds rolled in and intermittently obscured the quarter moon.

The tree canopy thickened. Something slithered through the nearby underbrush. I tried desperately to come up with a song in my head to shut out the rising panic, but all that came to mind was *Itsy-Bitsy Spider*.

I could really use a drink about now. And a case of bug spray.

My heart pounded so hard I just knew it was audible. Cold sweat trickled down my brow – and that's saying something for June in Texas.

No telling what I might step on out here. Or into. At this point, I wasn't opposed to it being more along the cow patty variety.

At least that crap wasn't alive.

I should've brought along a flashlight. Oh wait – my flashlight had been confiscated by good ol' Detective Duncan.

After this, I needed to pay him another visit and get my belongings back. I'm sure Bobby would like to have those letters returned too, even if they were the property of Amy's mother.

All thoughts of snakes, letters, and flashlights dissipated when a hand slapped over my mouth.

And stole my breath.

CHAPTER TWENTY-FOUR

The familiar hiss in my ear kept my bladder in check.

Mostly.

"What the hell are you doing here?"

Attempts at talking around firmly planted fingers proved futile until he let go and spun me around. In the near pitch-black darkness, it took a moment for my eyes to adjust and confirm what my ears had revealed.

"You didn't have to scare me like that," I replied.

"I guess calling out in the dark and having you scream loud enough to wake the dead would've been so much better," Zeke retorted.

"It might!"

"Keep your voice down."

"You first."

Momentary silence told me I was getting the Big Z dagger stare. "I'll ask again, what are you doing here, Vic?"

"Same as you," I said. "Trying to help clear Bobby's name."

"Trying to clear…?" Zeke started, then turned away and raked his hands through his hair before spinning back around to face me. "I'm on an op here. This has nothing to do with your boyfriend."

"Friend who's a boy…er, guy," I corrected. "And if this doesn't have anything to do with Bobby, why the trip to Austin? Why the interest in Amy's father, who happens to share the same last name of a known drug cartel?"

"Go home," Zeke hissed through clenched teeth.

"I'm not stupid, you know."

"Your actions say otherwise."

Before I had the chance to offer up my own thoughts on the matter, my feet and head switched places. It happened so fast, I thought for a sec I was falling.

Until I landed like a sack of potatoes on a hard and sinewy shoulder with a grunt.

Mine, not the Ranger's. Zeke didn't even breathe hard and carried me effortlessly as he trudged up the path the way I'd come.

"Let me go, Zeke Taylor," I demanded. "I'll just walk back. I'll call your mother on you. I'll scream."

With that threat firmly under his belt, Zeke flipped me over and placed me back on unsure footing.

"You'll scream, huh? And ruin any chance of helping Bobby?"

"Ha. Called it."

A frustrated sigh. His, not mine.

Then arms snaked around my waist, and he pressed against me. Zeke's sultry tenor licked the closing gap between us.

I gulped when a zing hit my nether regions like a lightning bolt. My legs turned to pudding.

"I only want to keep you safe, Vic," he whispered, warm breath hot against my cheek.

All thoughts of spiders, snakes, and lizards – oh my – dissipated. I forgot about the broken sandal. Charlotte's web.

Bobby who?

All I wanted at that moment was Zeke's lips on mine. I raised my arms to wrap around his neck and leaned in for the kill.

A disembodied voice shattered the moment. *"We've got movement out here."*

"Roger that." With that, he released me and pointed down the lane toward the cars. "Home. Now."

I trotted after him, three steps to every one of his. "I'm not a dog you can order around, you know."

Now some might argue that point with a capital B.

But Zeke wasn't one of them. "You don't need to get involved here."

"Involved? I'm already involved," I sputtered. "I got involved when my apartment was terrorized, traumatized, and ostracized."

"Ostracized?"

"Well, that's more me *from* my apartment. I'm homeless now."

"You're not homeless. I told you, you can stay with me as long as you need." He took off crashing through the underbrush like a hungry bear.

Too bad my stomach was the one that rumbled. "My point is, I've got just as much right to find the creep who started all of this as you do."

No response.

I took that as a sign to continue. "I'm just gonna keep following you."

He whipped around, a tree branch nearly slapping him in the face. "Then stay behind me and don't get in our way."

Progress!

With my floppy sandal it was a little difficult to keep up with Zeke's long and sure strides. Somehow I managed to trip along to where he and a couple of his Ranger cohorts crouched at the edge of the tree line.

A fenced pasture stretched across the clearing, the scent of manure clinging to my olfactory senses. But the empty field didn't appear to be the focus of concentration.

Dim lights flickered across the way. The tramp of cow hooves against metal and soft lowing followed as two-by-two the herd exited the semi-trailer like a reversal of Noah's ark.

See? I'd listened on occasion in Sunday School.

"Why are we watching the cow patty parade?" I whispered.

A terse *shh* was all the reply I warranted. Guess I should've been grateful Zeke had allowed me to tag along instead of hog-tying and throwing me in the bed of his truck. So in appreciation for finally relenting with my little tagalong, I stayed silent.

For a bit. "Is this a cow poaching operation?"

Another *shh*.

Don't hate me. I'm a girl. There's only so long those of the fairer and feminine sex can go before we have to speak, or we'll burst like an overflowing dam. It's coded into our genetic makeup.

You gotta problem with it, talk to God.

Mosquitoes attacked my bare legs like Kamikaze bombers during World War II. Dinner was served – and *I* was the one on the menu.

I could feel the welts rise across my arms and legs. Then the itching started in earnest.

"If we stay out here much longer, I'll need a blood transfusion," I complained.

"Then go home," Zeke whispered-shouted.

My feasted-on fanny stayed put.

A few moments later, a diesel engine fired up and the rig slowly pulled away from the scene, leaving us sitting near a field of dazed and confused cattle.

With a holler and a shout, the two wranglers got into a black four-wheel-drive truck with highly polished chrome that gleamed red in the rig's taillights. A lighted roll bar lit up on top when the throaty roar signaled life.

As it drove in the rig's wake, it struck me as familiar. But then black trucks around these parts are about as common as mosquitoes in summer.

A couple of hand signals and whispered commands, then the gang of four moved forward as one, sliding between the fence rails until sneaking up to one of the newly arrived animals.

I stayed at the fence and watched as three of the team corralled the heifer and held her down, while Zeke pulled on a long glove-like sheath that reached all the way up to his shoulder. Then much to my dismay, his gloved arm disappeared into the backside of the poor protesting animal.

So gross.

After fishing around in regions I'd rather not think about, Zeke slid his arm away and inspected what he held in his hand. Murmurs of acknowledgement passed between the team before they let the old girl go to trot away.

Zeke once told me I was full of crap. I'd always assumed that was a bad thing.

But seeing how excited the guys were as they headed my way with a handful of steaming cow shit, do you think I was wrong in my assumption?

Don't answer that.

"Drugs?"

He finished toweling his hair then tossed the damp mass my way. "Yep."

"In a cow's ass?"

"Yep."

Once again, Zeke strutted around his apartment all bare chested after his shower. So. Not. Fair. Displaying rippled pecs and abs were an unfair home court advantage.

"But how do they keep them from pooping it out before they're across the border?" I asked.

"You gotta shove the packs of heroin wa-a-ay up their colon shortly before crossing."

I really didn't need the emphasis. Or a demonstration. 'Specially when he was holding Slinky.

"Then you corral them on this side of the border and wait for them to release it. Those wranglers will return in a couple of nights with high-powered flashlights to search for fresh cow pies."

"That's gross," I whined, and continued slathering on the calamine lotion to stem the itch my earlier shower hadn't taken away.

Being a mosquito sandwich wasn't a fun way to spend an evening, but it was better than my party with Charlotte's web. A little.

Maybe.

"Gives a whole new meaning to taking a shit," Zeke said with a smile.

I'd never understand boys and their fascination with bodily functions.

"So instead of drug mules, the Juarez family is using cows now?"

"It's nothing new. The cartels change up their delivery methods, but they always circle back around to the ones that work. For awhile they were even hiding coke in boxes of diapers."

"Another *crappy* method," I said with a snort. Then my bathroom humor tempered. "So how does knowing this help me help Bobby?"

"We're trying to track their people on this side of the border," Zeke said. "All the while, I'm still trying to connect the dots leading to Amy."

"Then why didn't you chase after the delivery rig and the wranglers? At least get a license plate of that black truck."

"We've got a line on them, but we're hoping they'll lead us to the bigger fish when they come to pick up their load of crap in a few days."

"Okay. Yeah. I get it."

Zeke sidled up and tugged me into his arms. "I had fun with you out there tonight."

"Hmm," was all that came to mind as the scent of his body wash swaddled my senses.

"We make a good team, you know."

With only his towel and my robe between us, my legs turned to the noodley variety. "Uh...huh?"

My knees buckled as he nipped at my ear. "You doing anything next Friday night?"

At that moment, I conjured up a whole bunch of things I could do to him Friday night.

Do. I mean *do* Friday night.

"I g-g-gotta work," I stuttered.

"Can you ask off?" Lips trailed along my neck.

I'd be willing to ask for the whole week off if he kept doing that. "I...I can try."

"Good."

I nearly toppled across the antler monstrosity he called a coffee table when Zeke released me.

"Seven-thirty," Zeke continued. "Governor's dinner. Wear a cocktail dress. Come sober."

With that, he headed to his bedroom and shut the door, leaving me flustered and frustrated. Instead of rethinking my abstinence resolve, I seriously considered taking up archery right about then.

Less chance of forensics tracing the killing arrow back to me.

CHAPTER TWENTY-FIVE

Monday morning came way too early.

Sleeping on the sofa at Zeke's place was quickly wearing out its welcome. I'd be better off living in my Vette for the next few weeks.

I've never understood how a man could function with only a few hours of sleep night after night, while I become a raging wad of bitchy after missing the standard eight hours.

While Zeke clanged and puttered around getting ready for work, I tugged the blanket up over my head and burrowed my face into the pillow.

Eventually the thundering stopped, the front door slammed, and I was left in blissful peace to return to the realm of fevered dreams of firm pecs and soft lips.

Until a knock on the door reverberated through the apartment.

Muttering words that would turn the sun blue, I threw aside the blanket and shoved my arms into the robe as I stomped to the door.

Detective Dingbat Duncan's sweaty mug reflected through the peephole. I slung the door open.

"Ranger Taylor isn't here," I snarled.

"I'm not here for Zeke," Duncan said.

Eyes traveled up and down my frame. I'm sure mine were bloodshot, with dark circles a raccoon mother would be proud of. My hair likely stuck out at all angles, with knots the size of Texas.

But it took a moment to realize Duncan wasn't concerned about those aspects of my appearance, as his eyes were fixed on a particular area of my anatomy. My hastily donned robe hung wide open in the middle, exposing the thin fabric of my nightgown and giving him a birds-eye view of God's bestowed accoutrements.

I jerked the robe edges together. "What do you want then, Detective, besides to leer at me like a porn addict?"

His cheeks flushed.

Did I call it, or did I call it?

"You need to get dressed and come with me."

I folded my arms. "Why?"

"You've got some explaining to do."

"Explaining? About what?"

"How about providing misleading information to law enforcement?"

"What misleading information?"

"There's also hindering an official police investigation."

"In what way?" I demanded.

"Withholding evidence for starters."

"Hey, you can access the vital statistics information just as easily as I did."

"I'm talking about the text you sent to Amy Vernet the night she died."

Bitchiness died in my throat. "Text? What text?"

"This text." Duncan held a paper up to my face.

I nearly sucked all the air from Zeke's apartment as my mouth hung open like a sprung trapdoor. The exchange supposedly between my phone and Amy's stared from the page. Legs barely supported me, and I felt faint as I read the words.

Phantom Me: Need to talk. Can you meet at my apartment?
Amy: Certainly. When?
Phantom Me: Thirty minutes?
Amy: I'll be there.

The rest was Phantom Me sending directions to my place. Timestamps of the exchange reflected the later stage of my shift at the bar, though for the life of me I couldn't focus on exactly what had occurred that night.

The implication in the exchange, however, was crystal clear.

Though I tried to project a wall of confidence, my voice still sounded small. "I was at work until three like I told you before. I drove around the corner from my building and saw the lights that night. My boss can corroborate when I left. My b-b...friend Nick can too."

Even in the throes of trying to save my sorry carcass, I still couldn't call Nick my boyfriend. Regardless, Nick needed to get home from whatever modeling gig he was at – pronto.

For more reasons than one now.

Think about it.

"I still need you to get dressed and come down to the station," Duncan directed. "Oh, and I'll need to confiscate your phone as evidence."

In a daze, I let the detective into Zeke's apartment, feeling more than uncomfortable by his close proximity, not to mention this new information that made me look more involved than I already was.

A text? From my phone to Amy's? Was Duncan setting me up? Was this a ruse to try and get me to confess to something I hadn't done?

I went into this to help Bobby. But it appeared in the process I'd ended up with a target on my back.

With a sleight-of-hand worthy of a notorious pickpocket, I slid my cell between the clothes I'd laid out on Zeke's coffee table the night before, picked the bunch up, and headed toward the bathroom.

"I need to change, so I'll only be a minute."

Duncan grunted in acknowledgment before I closed the door, dropped the clothes on the counter, then fished out my phone. I prayed Zeke wasn't in some meeting or too far away to rescue this damsel in distress.

Just when I thought voice mail was ready to kick in, Zeke's voice came through loud and clear. "So Sleeping Beauty decided to wake up?"

"Yeah," I whispered. "But Sleeping Beauty needs Prince Charming to hightail it back to the castle before a dragon named Duncan hauls her off to jail."

No questions. No teasing. Not even a pause this time. "Stall. I'll be there in five."

There are perks to being a woman. To us five minutes is merely a suggestion and not an accurate measurement of the clock.

Sleeping Beauty delayed as long as possible, keeping the water running while washing my face, brushing my teeth and hair, and just plain covering up the sound of my knocking knees.

Prince Charming, on the other hand, must've broken every traffic law on the books to arrive within a measurable five minute window after ending the call. Sometimes it really paid to carry a badge.

Duncan scowled and was none too happy to see Zeke storm the castle.

"Watching my place to see when I'd leave?" Zeke asked, eyes blazing.

"Must've just missed you," Duncan returned with a little less confidence than before.

"I thought we had an agreement, Duncan."

"Agreement?" I questioned. "What agreement?"

Without looking away from zeroing in on the detective, Zeke responded to my question. "The agreement Detective Duncan and I had that he would contact me if he had any further questions for you."

What was this? *Dick Measuring 101* again?

That did it. I was sick of being fought over, fawned about, and frisky. Or was that frisked?

Regardless, anger sizzled like a vat of hot oil. My french fries were beyond crispy now. We're talking black as hockey pucks.

"Seriously?" I growled, forgetting one was there to save me from a one-way trip to the slammer. "I'm sick and tired of you guys trying to corral me for your own purposes. I'm not like those cows from last night."

I pointed out my frustrations in turn. "First Zeke here is trying to get me back in his bed, and now Detective Dingbat here shows up to leer at me. What's next from you, Duncan? Planning to frisk me so you can *cop* a feel?"

The accidental double-entendre was merely icing on the cake.

The mere mention of cake sent my stomach into *feed me* mode. I wasn't going anywhere or with anyone until I got some nourishment. Caffeine for starters.

While I stomped off into the kitchen to take advantage of pre-percolated fuel, Duncan showed Zeke the written trail of my phantom text conversation with Amy.

For all I knew, this was just a ploy by the desperate detective to try and come up with a motive for Amy's murder. As if Bobby and I were lovers or something and had offed his wife together.

I froze.

The coffee pot trembled in my hand as I tried not to send it on a shattering trajectory. Bobby and I had a known history. With a police report to back it up.

It didn't require too much of a stretch of the imagination to conclude Bobby could've filled his wife with enough sleeping pills to put down a horse. Then I lured Amy to my building where I tossed her to the asphalt parking lot below. Then Bobby and I lived happily ever after.

It made sense in a twisted sort of way. At least from the detective's warped perspective. Only one problem.

Not a bit of it was true, not to mention the other holes in the theory.

How would a sleeping-pill filled Amy have driven halfway across town without falling asleep at the wheel?

Ignoring that little anomaly, how would either of us have thrown her over the side without leaving any footprints along the asphalt rooftop?

Then again, how would I have gained access to the roof in the first place without a key to unlock the door?

The detective's entire theory was predicated on the possibility I'd sent Amy a series of text messages.

Damning test messages.

I put down the coffee pot, strode across the living room and grabbed my phone from the bathroom while the local law enforcement twins argued over jurisdiction of my residency. A careful scroll through the history to that night.

Oh yeah, wet t-shirt night. Fake Boobs had won, though I'd commandeered much of the attention during the awards ceremony that night. A night when I'd been briefly separated from my phone to protect it from the elements.

A shock shivered down my spine as I stared at the text evidence on my phone. Evidence that could fry me like a french fry. But at least now I had a better idea of how all this was connected.

And a good idea who the nefarious culprit was.

CHAPTER TWENTY-SIX

After Duncan grudgingly re-upped the agreement with Zeke for my responsibility, they both left for greener pastures.

The rest of Monday I spent in my bathrobe, hiding out from the gathering storm like the yellow-livered filly I was.

Of that, I had no trouble admitting. I was so scared at that point, you may as well have treated me for yellow fever. Or jaundice.

Instead of sleeping off the late night and too early morning, I alternated between planning how I'd trip the cowardly killer into a confession and the desire to hide beneath my mother's skirts like when I was a girl.

Okay, you got me.

Since I was never really the hiding type, that left me with coordinating my counterpoint to his point. Thus far the killer had been successful at keeping suspicion at bay. He'd pointed the finger not only Bobby's direction, but mine as well.

But in so doing, he'd given himself away.

When I woke up Tuesday morning, I faced an exhausting day of shopping with Mom, who even allowed restocking of some of my rather scandalous attire for bartending duty.

There's something to be said for Momma Bear Syndrome.

She also wrangled it out of me about Friday's planned attendance of the governor's dinner on Zeke's arm. Which, after that confession, required yet another visit to another store, one of Mom's favorite and exclusive boutiques.

Personally, I thought she'd developed visions of grandchildren with my pronouncement, even though I insisted I'd been strong-armed into agreeing to go with the Ranger.

At the end of the day, not only were my dogs barking but the sperm donor's bank account had to be howling like a hound dog at a full moon.

Between Monday's planning and Tuesday's spending, by Wednesday evening I was all set to lasso me a killer. But do you remember what they say about those best laid plans of mice and men?

Yeah, this mouse forgot that tidbit too.

The parking lot at the bar was sparsely populated when I pulled in, but one black truck with a lighted roll bar over the cab grabbed my attention.

Check one – the bird was in the nest.

My legs went all noodley as I walked across the lot. But instead of attraction to my boss, this time it was fear that had me in a near swoon.

I had to hold it together to get through a shift without revealing I was onto him. Would I be able to play our little *tete-a-tete* with the usual sexy and sophisticated aplomb?

Okay fine. I wasn't so sophisticated, but I could still play the sexy part.

So check two – the yeller-livered filly was cured of jaundice.

Well, maybe not cured, but definitely on the mend.

I think.

Check three, however, screeched to a halt like the Vette stopping on a dime when I entered the bar.

"What the hell are you doing here? Where's Grady?"

Bud stopped prepping and offered up a wink. "Grady called and asked me to come in for him tonight."

"Then why's his truck out in yonder parking lot?" I inquired.

"That's a Chevy, not a Dodge," Bud replied with a smirk. "Square wheel wells, not round. It's my brand new baby."

"At least it got you here before me for once." I tossed my purse into a cabinet.

Bud grunted. "Since it was an emergency the other job let me off early."

I should've noticed the wheel well shapes. Already the night wasn't going as planned, which had the gray matter spinning as to how to accommodate this unexpected hiccup.

"Well don't try and sneak off early from *this* job then," I said.

Clean glasses sat in the top rack of the dishwasher. I grabbed a towel and started drying, half disappointed and half relieved that I wouldn't have to face the boss.

Which meant I wouldn't get any answers tonight either.

"What was Grady's emergency?" I asked my co-worker.

"Said he wasn't feeling well. Probably went home to hork up a hairball," Bud replied with a laugh.

"Ugh, thanks for the visual. I know all about hairballs."

"Yeah, I've heard those long-haired cats can be especially nasty."

My insides clenched and the glass almost slipped from my fingers. "H-how do you know about my cat?"

Shields went up and Bud's eyes grew hooded. Guarded. "Well uh…you talk about that mangy feline enough around here."

"Oh," I replied, noting his fake Texas accent slipped.

Tension thickened. Silence between us extended as I lined the shelf with glass after glass. My mind whirled with conflicting thoughts as the band came in and warmed up for the night. I smiled as usual when patrons ordered.

All the while my brain buzzed with something other than beer.

As far as I could remember, Slinky had never been a topic of conversation in the workplace. Even if something had slipped between my inebriated lips, I doubt the length of my tabby's fur would've been the memorable highpoint of anyone's night.

So where would Bud have come across that information but through firsthand knowledge? And how would he have come across that knowledge unless he'd been in my apartment?

Uninvited.

Trust me. Bud would've never been *invited* to my apartment, no matter how drunk as a skunk I got.

That left me with only one conclusion – Bud had been to my apartment without my knowledge.

He'd seen my pet. Threatened my sweet baby kitty. Stowed the critter away in my closet and ransacked my rooms.

That realization swung me between rage and fear like a hyperactive pendulum.

Now it made sense why Grady kept Bud's worthless and lazy ass around. Why he put up with the constant tardiness and early escape. Loyalty to an old Army buddy had nothing to do with it.

Grady and Bud were partners on this side of the cartel's drug smuggling operation.

Since Zeke knew Grady a bit, I hadn't wanted to bring him in on my plans to try and trip up the boss tonight. But did Zeke know about Grady's nefarious connections?

If Grady and Bud were the wranglers we'd seen at the cattle pasture the other night, the Ranger had to have been onto them. Zeke had even said they had a line on identities but were waiting for them to lead authorities to the bigger fish in the pond.

And I'd worked side-by-side with those two rotten, stinkin', bottom feeders for years.

No, Zeke didn't realize who Grady really was, or he'd never have allowed me to work at this particular bar.

Not that I'd have paid much attention to Zeke's cautions or demands, mind you. You should know by now that I'm not very good with ultimatums.

The only questions still in need of adequate answers were not only why Amy was killed by the cartel after all these years, but why they tried to pin her death on Bobby. And why use my phone to draw Amy to my apartment in the first place?

The answers might be as mundane as a convenient means to an end, all the way up to me being the intended target all along, what with all the activity centered on my building.

Hey, I know I'm a bit narcissistic and all, but that's a plausible suspicion when you're the only child of a well-known and wealthy family.

It could also explain why my apartment was vandalized instead of burglarized when they discovered I was *in absentia*. Then again, Grady knew I'd be gone to Austin with Zeke that day.

Damn. I'd really wanted some answers tonight, but now I was more confused than ever.

The only things I was sure of were drug smuggling goings on, Amy's biological father connected to a drug cartel, and Bobby charged with Amy's murder.

And somehow my boss and co-worker were involved.

One of them corresponded with Amy from my phone. One of them tore apart my apartment. And one of them threw Amy off my building without leaving any footprints.

Footprints.

I'd forgotten all about checking the roof. As soon as I escaped tonight, I needed to see if the access door in my building was unlocked. Then I could get a bird's-eye view of what Amy had seen of the Dallas skyline before someone else sent her on her journey.

Spirits lifted, I finished the night alongside a potential killer and skedaddled across the parking lot as fast as my cowardly-lion legs would carry me. Bud was still halfway to his truck when I fired up the Vette and peeled out toward home.

Ah, home.

The old brick building had never looked as good as it did when I pulled into the parking lot. I missed having my own space to crawl home to every night.

Since I'd given my only key to Mom, I couldn't step inside to check out what direction Reggie had taken the décor of my apartment. But after only a few days, there probably wasn't much to see 'cept perhaps new paint on the walls. Special order takes weeks. Sometimes months.

I groaned – and not from the extra floors required to scale the building to the top.

The sixth floor roof access door had a shiny new padlock in place, likely installed after I'd made Jimmy-the-Super mad with my accusations.

Hmm, I'd kinda forgotten all about where Jimmy fit into the picture now that Grady and Bud were the prime suspects. Was he actually involved somehow? Maybe he was the muscle.

If so, I hoped he hadn't heard me come through the front door. Perhaps he'd think I'd come home for more clothes for my extended sleepover. Or that I'd forgotten about the state of my place while in a drunken haze.

Hey, don't judge.

A closer inspection revealed the padlock wasn't the problem. The brass plate screwed into the door jamb appeared loose, as if the screws were stripped.

Using a fingernail, I easily slid first one then another screw from the soft wood until a tug of the plate sent the remaining screws falling into my palm and the door swinging open with a drawn-out spooky creak.

Thank God it wasn't near Halloween or I'd have been close to piddling my panties again.

First the visit with Charlotte at her web and now creaky doors. Instead of laying off the sex, maybe it was time to abstain from the horror movies for awhile.

Ya think?

A summer breeze whispered across the threshold as I stood in the doorway and surveyed the surrounds. The bright lights of downtown flickered in the not-so-far distance, providing enough ambient light with which to make out the nearby air conditioning units churning out cold air to the apartments below.

My heels sunk ever so slightly as I stepped onto the rubber covered asphalt surface and walked to the first unit. I flicked on the new flashlight I'd bought and looked at the imprints left in my wake.

Yep, definite evidence of shoe impressions.

The killer could've walked along the units to the wide concrete edge to avoid leaving footprints across the roof. But that still didn't explain why there was nothing between the doorway and the first unit.

A big heavy man carrying a petite but pregnant woman? Yeah, footprints left behind for sure.

Unless…

The idea struck out of left field. I removed my new pumps anyway and set them carefully along the edge of an air conditioner. The rubberized asphalt was still warm from the hot summer sun but not too uncomfortable on my bare feet this time of night as I returned to the door. The flashlight beam revealed what I'd hoped not to see.

Bare foot imprints. Barely there, but there nonetheless.

I hung my head with a sigh – and caught sight of a sliver of wood behind the open door. A tug sent the door creaking again and revealed a narrow slab of plywood leaning within reach against the wall.

The weathered wood looked just long enough to create a pathway across the roof between the door and the first air conditioning unit. With a long stride – easy for a taller man – once he got to the first, it'd be a simple matter of hopping from one unit to the next over to the edge.

But you'd have to have really good balance to walk around the cement edge to the parking lot side where Amy's body was found.

The heat of a Texas day caused any shoe imprints in the rubber lining to dissipate over time, evidenced by the lack of

Jimmy's impressions from when he'd come up on the roof to work. Heavy boot imprints would sink down pretty deep, though. However, my barefoot imprints hardly showed.

If the killer decided to go barefoot and *did* falter while balancing a pregnant woman in his arms, he may have stepped down from the edge somewhere on his journey and left a mark the police missed.

I started to tiptoe to the end of the units to follow-up on the idea and left my shoes behind. Being barefoot allowed me to be discrete and not leave behind too much of my own trail if Duncan decided to continue harassing me.

Being barefoot also helped the killer creep across the rooftop without making a sound – a realization I had right about the time I was grabbed from behind and a hand slammed across my mouth.

CHAPTER TWENTY-SEVEN

Unfortunately for me, the man-handling wasn't from Zeke this time.

"You think you're always so smart," Bud whispered in my ear, stale beer breath hot on my cheek. "Got your rich mommy and daddy to bail you out so you can play instead of work a real job, while people like me have to work two."

My scream was muffled and the metallic taste of blood seeped past my lips. I tried to wrench my pinned arms from Bud's meat hook, but all that got me was pressed up tighter against him.

It was immediately obvious my struggles turned the creep on.

"Flirting with every guy you see," he continued. "Letting them feel you up."

Warm slobbery lips dipped to my neck and sent my heart racing into overdrive. 'Cept this time it was from disgust.

In a swift takedown, Bud swept my feet out from beneath me, grinding my knees and face into the roof to where I could barely breathe, much less scream, as he sat on top of me and secured my wrists with a zip tie.

That was gonna leave more than just a mark.

My eyes watered, blurring my view of the nearby roof edge where Amy had last stood.

"Humping everyone except me, Vicki. Why is that?"

Before I could answer or scream, Bud stuffed an oily rag in my mouth. The crushing weight lifted only long enough for him to flip me to my side, one hand trailing up my leg while the other grabbed my breast.

My stomach clenched. I cringed as the little I'd eaten that day threatened to come up.

Bud moaned until I succeeded in kicking him in the leg. But at that angle I couldn't get any power behind the thrust, and it probably came across more like a pat of encouragement to him.

Bud laughed and gripped my breast until it hurt like a punch to the gut. "Still think you're too good for me? My dick could fill you up more than that sissy pretty boy you've been shacking up with."

I was pretty sure he meant Nick and not my current roomie. Uh, landlord. Er...

Oh hell, I didn't know what to call Zeke. I just wished one of the guys in my orbit would ride in at that moment like the cavalry and save me.

Wait a sec. I was no shrinking damsel. In distress? Sure, but not some ditzy dame who couldn't take care of herself.

While Bumbling Bud had been talking and taking advantage, I'd used my tongue to work the rag loose until I spit it out in his face. Sometimes it helps having a tangoing tongue that gets regular workouts.

Or a big mouth.

"Get your hands off me," I screamed, "or so help me you won't have a dick left to piss with."

As he grabbed for the rag, I sat up and caught him right in the nose with a crack. I saw stars, while the howl he let loose would've rivaled a hellhound.

Blood gushed down his shirtfront as I scrambled to my feet and dashed toward the door like a wingless chicken. His hand clamped down and spun me around to face the edge once again.

"You just can't leave well enough alone," Bud snarled as he shoved a gun under my chin and dragged me toward the cement surround.

"Stop right there!"

My hero stood in the roof entrance doorway in the form of one Jimmy-the-Super, his white boxers gleaming in the dark. A gun wavered in his two-fisted grip, and my heart lurched as Bud used me as a human shield.

With Jimmy's drooping right side, it made me wonder which of us he held in his sights. Not a pleasant thought in this situation, but it was nice to see I'd been wrong about my landlord's employee.

"Let her go," Jimmy demanded.

Bud barely flinched when he flicked his gun barrel from my chin toward the super. The report rang in my ears as Jimmy fell backward in a heap on the landing, his return shot going high and wide.

The cavalry's ride was over before it had even mounted. My hero lay dying.

I was next.

The scent of singed flesh joined that of spent gunpowder when Bud shoved the smoking barrel against my neck. Tears ran warm down my cheeks, but I refused to give my captor the pleasure of crying out in pain.

Instead I pulled out the only weapon I had left in my arsenal – talking him to death.

LOOK BEFORE YOU JUMP

Being a woman does have its advantages.

"Did you try to rape Amy too before you tossed her over the side?" I asked, trying to delay while I thought up a new plan of escape.

"A pregnant woman?" Bud spat. "How desperate do you think I am?"

"Pretty desperate to kill her. The only thing I wonder is why."

"You're so smart, you tell me."

You know? It's amazing how near death brings about absolute clarity.

"The cartel," I huffed, digging in my bare feet to the soft rooftop. "Amy's father is part of the Juarez drug cartel."

I think that surprised him, as Bud stopped for a sec. "So?"

"And you're part of their drug smuggling operation. I saw you and Grady unloading the cattle the other night."

That little revelation sent him into overdrive. "You don't know nothin'."

"Like I didn't know Amy's death wasn't a suicide?"

Bud grunted. "If you'd have just shut up, the cops would've never reopened the case. It's your fault I had to plant the sleeping pill bottle at that sniveling preacher's house."

That got my dander up. "For your information, that sniveling preacher is my friend."

I raised my bare foot and brought the full weight of my heel down on his toes. That only served to make him mad. In my fear-induced stupor, I kinda forgot I'd left my spiky-heeled weapons near the air conditioners.

Instead of pulling the trigger, Bud cold cocked me with the gun butt. The stars in the sky started swirling as if God had sped up the earth's rotation.

My body went weightless, as if flung toward outer space, at the same time a second gun report echoed in the night and the ground rose up to meet me.

But instead of hard, unforgiving cement, my body flopped against rubber-covered asphalt. Then my head found the cement edge.

Through the fog, I looked up into a familiar face. The warm chocolate gaze soothed my insides as I realized my mistake. One side of his mustache tipped up like a salute of greeting as he lifted my head.

"How ya doing, Vic?"

"Been better, Grady."

The stars spun tighter around his face in a candy-coated kaleidoscope of color.

Then I blacked out.

CHAPTER TWENTY-EIGHT

Once again, my apartment building swarmed with red and blue lights. Only this time they weren't there for a dead body.

Well, 'cept Bud's.

Somewhere among my in-and-out consciousness, I heard Grady's bullet had been an amazing one-in-a-million shot. Got 'im right between the eyes. Stopped Bud's momentum cold just as he was about to hurl me off the roof.

Sirens wailed into the night as the first ambulance on scene herded Jimmy toward the hospital. Grady assured me he would be alright.

The bullet near his shoulder was a clean through-and-through, nothing surgery and plenty of rest couldn't repair. The fall down the stairwell, however, earned him a date with a CAT scanner.

With a wave of the hand, Grady shooed away the paramedics and sat beside my gurney in the second ambulance.

"An undercover ATF agent?" I asked over the clanging in my head.

"Shh," Grady hushed. "Not so loud."

"Why didn't you tell me?"

"Uh, undercover for a reason."

Oh. Right.

The scrambled pieces of my brain hadn't yet congealed together enough to wade through something as mundane as a logical conversation.

"Does Zeke know?"

"Sure," Grady returned. "Who do you think recommended ya for the job?"

I groaned and laid back against the hard pillow. "So who recommended Bud for the job, huh?"

A frown drew Grady's mustache down. "That really did start out as an attempt to help an old Army buddy. Wasn't until a few months after I'd hired Bud that I suspected more was up with his other job. That's when I pulled in Ranger Taylor."

"So what about your Army buddy now?"

"Yeah, that's gonna be a hard call. Really wish I hadn't had to put Bud's name on that bullet."

I put a hand over Grady's. "Sorry to have put you through the trouble."

He patted mine. "I'd do it all over again to save ya, Vic."

Before I could say anything else, Zeke's wide-eyed gaze filled my tear-blurred vision. "Vicki?"

"Zeke," I cried, sending my clattering brain running for cover.

His gaze traveled over every bruise and blister, scratch and scrape before lifting my chin to check out the salved and gauze covered wound on my neck. Brown eyes asked the question his mouth wouldn't – or couldn't – say.

"Just a small burn," I reassured. "From Bud's gun muzzle. I'll be fine."

Zeke grunted then offered a single curt nod Grady's direction. "Grady."

"Zeke," Grady responded.

"Many thanks for saving our girl," Zeke said.

"Someone had to protect her ass." Grady chuckled. "Though I'm still tryin' to figure out some way to steal her away from ya."

"Hey," I butt in. "Nobody's stealing nothing from somebody's ass."

Wait a sec. That didn't come out right. Let's try this again.

"I'm an unattached woman. End of story."

"Speaking of stories," Grady said, "I caught that last bit Bud said about planting the sleeping pills at the Vernet house."

"Yeah? Well, you can hear the whole story if you want." I lifted my blouse and jimmied the mic loose from my bra before handing it over to Grady. "That is, if the recorder in my car was still on."

Two sets of eyes darted toward then away from my exposed assets so fast, I would've laughed if my head wasn't already begging for mercy.

Zeke offered a hike of his brow instead of a furrow this time. "Recorder?"

I nodded – then regretted it. "See, the other day I stopped by this electronics store and picked up a few things. I used the tracking device the other night to find you, Zeke."

The brow hike immediately dove south with his frown. "I discovered it after I got home."

"Then I was gonna question Grady here tonight," I said, thumbing my boss. "Until I got there and realized Bud was also involved and it turns out my boss is actually a…" I lowered my voice to a whisper this time. "…an ATF agent."

Grady's mustache lifted on both sides this time. "I'll let ya interrogate me anytime, Vic."

I smiled, though with the pain in my head, side, legs, knees, neck – oh hell, pretty much my entire body – my grin probably came out more like a grimace.

"Does this mean Bobby's officially off the hook?"

"I think that's a safe bet," Grady responded.

I sighed and settled into the gurney. "Okay then. How about you guys go away now and let me get some well-deserved sleep?"

"I'm afraid that won't be possible," the female paramedic said as she climbed into the ambulance. "With the head trauma, we need to get you fully checked out at the hospital to ensure there's not a concussion. That means you've gotta stay awake."

Damn. Why couldn't I have stayed unconscious a little longer?

Say 'til the cows came home.

Hours later, after plenty of poking, prodding, and a trip through the tube, peaceful sleep was allowed at last.

When Mom and Dad arrived at the emergency room, she insisted I be kept overnight for observation, even though scans showed no sign of a concussion.

Talk about overkill.

But I was glad I was still among the land of the living. So this cub was happy to acquiesce to the momma bear's demands.

For once.

By that point, *overnight* was rather a misnomer too since the sky had lightened by the time I was ushered into a private room. When I opened my eyes some hours later, the early evening sun had shifted right into my eyes and sent my headache into overdrive again.

Figures.

The scent of food woke my brain – and my stomach – up further. Mom sat at a nearby table with Janine, daintily eating dinner from styrofoam containers. If I'd have had a camera, the scene would've been worthy of a Kodak moment.

You know. Fodder to tease my mom with later when I felt better.

'Cause I couldn't remember ever seeing my mother eat from anything but the finest china. Add in the plastic fork, and I nearly laughed my ass right off the bed.

Internally, of course.

My low chuckles drew their attention anyway. Plastic forks took a dive into styrofoam before they hovered by the bed in two seconds flat.

"How're you feeling?" Mom and Janine asked at the same time.

"Like I almost got tossed off a building," I mumbled.

Janine's blue eyes widened at the same Mom's green narrowed. "*Almost* being the key word in this situation," Mom said. "Let's stay focused on the positive."

"What happened?" Janine asked.

"Long story," I said with a groan when I tried to raise my head. "Let's just say I no longer have to worry about a certain co-worker pawing at me again."

Mom released a sharp humph before addressing me. "Your boss…I believe his name was Grady?"

I nodded then closed my eyes to keep the room from spinning like I was riding the tilt-a-whirl at the fair.

"He asked me to inform you that you have the remainder of the week off. With combat pay, whatever that means."

"Good ol' Grady."

Now that I knew he had not just one but *two* income streams, I wasn't ashamed to accept the paid time off, though I knew it meant more work for my remaining cohorts at the bar. Considering my injuries came at someone else's expense, I hoped they wouldn't hold it against me.

After I finished convalescing though, I'd have to check in with Grady to see what I could and couldn't say about the night's activities. He had a secret identity to protect, you know.

Like Batman.

Janine piped up. "Bobby should be by anytime to check in on you again."

That opened my eyes again right quick. "Was he here earlier?"

My best friend nodded. "He wanted to let you know Detective Duncan contacted him this morning to inform him that he could expect charges to be dropped once the DA's office filed the formal paperwork."

"Yes!"

I shot my bandaged arm up into the air and almost caught Janine's chin with my right hook. The throbbing in my skull lessened about the time I almost shared the love with my best friend.

Mom interrupted our celebration. "I still don't understand why Bobby asked you to get involved in the first place."

"Don't worry about it, Mom. Chalk it up to a friend helping a friend. You know, because of my connection with Zeke?"

I hoped the simple explanation would placate the momma bear so she'd let her cub off the hook without any further questions. And really, it was only a friend helping a friend.

Mostly.

Sorta.

Truth be told, I'd found the little adventure rather exciting. Well, 'cept for the part about almost taking a swan dive from my rooftop.

"Speaking of Zeke," Mom continued, "he said to let him know as soon as the hospital released you."

"He said you could have the bed tonight too," Janine included.

I doubt if she realized the implications of the sentence until it was out of my bestie's mouth. The blush brightened Janine's face so fast, a bystander flying past the window might've mistaken it for a hot flash.

"I'll keep that in mind," I returned with a wink.

Mom just shook her head and headed for the hall. "I'm going to step out and call your father to let him know you're awake."

"Where is the old so-and-so?" I asked Janine after the door clicked shut. "I could've sworn he was here last night, acting like a concerned parent. So unlike him."

"He stayed until I left to get dinner from the cafeteria."

"That long? Probably waiting to see if he could take me out of the will permanently this time."

"Vicki," Janine admonished. "Have you ever considered that this was a wake-up call for him? Your dad really did seem quite concerned about you."

The sperm donor concerned about me? There's a new one.

I wasn't quite sure how to feel about the emotion that thought churned up in my gut, so I decided to file it away under rainy day contemplations for the New Year. Like sometime around 2050. Maybe by then I'd be mature enough to handle it.

Or not.

Further consideration at present was cut short by Bobby's entrance with an enormous plant.

"Vic?" His eyes widened when he got a good look at me around the flora and fauna. "Dear Father in Heaven!"

In my extensive experience, such a reaction from a man was never a good sign.

"Do I look worse than earlier?" I asked, searching for a mirror or any reflective surface.

"Sorry. You look, uh…fine."

"Okay Pinocchio. Don't start lying to me now." My gaze shifted between Janine biting her lip and Bobby's concerned stare. "How bad is it?"

He hesitated. "Remember that little altercation you had with Lorraine Padget the summer before you started high school?"

"Ye-ea-ah-h?" I said drawing it out to stall the inevitable.

Bobby smiled and shrugged. "At least this time you only have one black eye."

After a good groan, I proceeded to share the circumstances about the case and the demise of Amy's killer. The one question I still couldn't answer adequately left us all hanging.

What was the real reason Amy had been targeted after all these years?

CHAPTER TWENTY-NINE

Okay, so I was a little beat-up, bruised, and burned. But that was no reason to miss the governor's dinner. I just did what any resourceful Texas woman would do.

Improvised.

"Your mom bought that for you, didn't she?" Zeke asked when I stepped from his bathroom in the black cocktail dress.

"Maybe," I replied.

He chuckled and stuck out his elbow for me to slip my arm through. "In all my years of knowing you, Vic, I've never seen you with that much skin, um...covered."

I smacked his arm and looked again at the dress in the elevator door's reflection. The clingy modal and spandex fabric fell well below the knee to hide most of the assorted scuffs and scrapes on my legs.

The long lace sleeves helped break up the appearance of asphalt and rubber-induced burn marks along my elbows and arms, though the sleeves held in the heat and served to exacerbate the itching.

There wasn't a whole lot I could do about the gun muzzle burn on my neck and the bruises on my face, but the thick cover-up Mom had provided did a fairly decent job of toning it down somewhat.

Wearing my hair cascading down helped a bit too, which was probably what made the Ranger sit up and take notice on the drive to the venue.

If Zeke was embarrassed to be seen with me in public, he did a pretty good job of masking it when we walked into the sparsely-populated ballroom. Since he was technically on duty tonight, we'd had to arrive a bit ahead of the crowd.

But while he left to confer with the other Rangers in preparation for the governor's arrival, I found it quite enjoyable to sit by and watch the parade of tuxes and assorted frippery as guests entered.

The parents eventually came strolling in with Mr. and Mrs. De'Laruse, my mother targeting in like a laser beam on where I sat at the bar. After the required greetings all around, Mom made a beeline in my direction as I wobbled to stand.

"Do you think it's wise to be drinking alcohol after a head injury, Victoria? You're still taking the pain killers the doctor prescribed, aren't you?"

I shook the ice in my nearly empty glass. "Ginger ale won't kill me, Mom."

"Oh. Well. Perhaps that blow to the head knocked a little sense into you after all," she quipped with a gentle hug. Mom then held me at arm's length. "And what did I tell you about that dress? Makeup covered those bruises quite nicely also. If not for the swelling, you'd look stunning, dear."

Gee, thanks for the backhanded compliments there, Mom.

Instead I held my ginger ale to hers with a soft plink. "As usual you did good, though Zeke thinks the dress covers too much skin."

That got me a humph. "Where is that young man anyway? He should've never left you alone here. That's no way to treat an escort on a proper date."

"It's not a date, Mom," I admonished. "Besides, Zeke's working security detail tonight. I doubt if I'll see him much."

"Well, I still don't think…"

Mom's comment was interrupted by the start-up of the band and the entrance of the governor and his entourage. With a quick peck, she excused herself and went in search of my dad in the press of the crowd.

Her concern over my being left in the dust by the Ranger was rather touching though.

Unable to handle anymore bodily injury, I avoided the jostling and jockeying for position and started on my second ginger ale. What I wouldn't give for a big, tall, frothy mug of beer.

Better yet, a shot or two of Jack.

About halfway through the cocktail hour, I was whirled around off my stool and swept onto the dance floor. When my head stopped spinning, I looked up into Zeke's brown eyes.

"You might want to take it easy on the twirling," I admonished, "or you might be wearing dinner *before* I eat it."

"Apologies, milady," he quipped. Then sobered. "We just haven't danced together in a long time, and I…" He cleared his throat as if nervous around me. "I've, uh…kinda been looking forward to this."

"I thought tonight was all business."

"I've learned to multi-task."

He spun me out and then brought me back into his arms without missing a beat.

"And to dance properly," I observed.

Not that the guy would ever be Fred Astaire. Still, color me impressed.

"I had to have something to do with all that spare time after you left and I was no longer tied up chasing you all the time."

"You calling me a time suck?"

"Among other things," Zeke growled.

Uh-oh. I knew that growl – and it wasn't from anger. It didn't take too much stretch to imagine how he mistook my meaning.

"So," I said in attempt to change the subject. "Why did you ask me to your little Ranger soiree? You can't be that hard up for a date."

The heated and devilish grin had me rethinking my disease-ridden mouth at the poor choice of words. Maybe I *had* suffered a concussion or something the other night.

Yeah, I hear you. *Or something* is right.

Blame it on the pain pills for taking the edge off my gray matter.

Zeke pressed the earwig against his ear and spoke into his sleeve. Then he glanced over his shoulder and swirled me off the dance floor.

"I asked you," Zeke said as he pressed me to his side and wove through the adulating throng, "because there's someone here I think you'd like to meet."

"I'll give you a kiss here and now if you say *Sam Adams*."

"A beer is the last thing you need right now, but I think you'll appreciate the substitution."

Now let me 'splain something here.

When you've been around the block of power and prestige so many times since you stopped wearing training panties, a meeting with the governor of the great State of Texas ranked right up there with cleaning the cookies out of your critter's litterbox.

Therefore, when he'd entered the room earlier, I'd paid less attention to him and more salivating over the beer line-up I couldn't have.

Damnit.

So when the Hispanic gentleman standing near our fearless leader came into focus, my heart skipped a beat.

The rather petite and slender frame appeared even smaller next to Zeke's towering height. The full lips displayed the practiced smile of a politician, but the dark eyes turned down at the corners.

Something about him drew me in – and seemed vaguely familiar.

Zeke made introductions. "Victoria Bohanan, may I present Mr. Julio Benito Juarez, Mexican Ambassador to the United States."

Sad eyes perked up at the introduction, while my heart skipped a beat. I glanced from Zeke to the ambassador before I remembered my manners and stuck out my hand.

"It's a pleasure to meet you, Ambassador Juarez."

He also quickly looked back and forth between me and Zeke for a sec before grasping my hand in both of his and placing a delicate kiss across my knuckles.

"*Seniorita* Bohanan, the pleasure is all mine. It is truly an honor."

"An honor, sir?"

Before I realized what was happening, Zeke spoke into his cuff and the three of us stepped through a sudden opening in the wall into a back hallway.

I was so stunned when Ranger Taylor then jogged to the end of the hall to give us privacy, I didn't even think to ask why he'd not only introduced me to a suspected drug lord but left me alone with him.

But fear and anger dissipated with the tears glistening in the ambassador's eyes. "I have so much to thank you for and so little time in which to do so."

"Th-thank me?" I stuttered.

"For clearing my son-in-law's name. For befriending my daughter, and placing yourself in harm's way to catch her killer."

I didn't even flinch when he drew my hair to the side to touch my neck near where the muzzle burn hid under the makeup.

I stared over his head at Zeke, who offered a barely discernable nod in return.

"I don't understand," I said to Ambassador Juarez. "Why kill Amy? She had nothing to do with the...family business."

Okay, I may be a little scatterbrained after the head trauma, but I'm not stupid.

I wasn't about to accuse the man standing in front of me of involvement in a less-than-reputable international enterprise.

"I've spent a lifetime distancing myself from the family trade," Juarez admitted to me. "I took great pains to hide my daughter's existence and keep our contact confidential. But someone in the family discovered my secret and used her to force my involvement. What with my political ties and all..." Juarez's voice drifted.

"Who tipped them off?" I asked. "Do you think it might've coincided with their mission activities in Central America?"

"That is what I intend to find out." Juarez's eyes hardened into obsidian disks. "With my daughter gone, my family now has no leverage against me. I plan to turn state's evidence against them to shut down the operation that has destroyed not only other families, but my own as well."

For once in my life I was speechless.

The ambassador offered a sad smile. "Now not only Ranger Taylor knows my intentions, but you also. I trust you will guard that knowledge?"

"I will, Mr. Ambassador," I promised, finally finding my voice again. "And thank you for sharing with me about your daughter. Amy was a joy to know."

Even if only for a brief moment.

"If you ever have need of my assistance, Miss Bohanan, you have but to call my direct line...as my daughter once did." He slipped a card from his wallet and handed it to me before touching my cheek. "I can see why she liked you."

Ambassador Juarez then swept from the hallway and returned to the awaiting party. I just stared at the door as it closed.

So many questions I had wanted to ask burbled through my brain. Then a realization crept over me like a swarm of spiders. For all Amy's talk of openness in her marriage, it seems she'd kept at least one secret from Bobby.

Her knowledge of and contact with her father.

Keeping him a secret made sense in a way though. 'Specially considering how much the senior Vernets already despised Amy.

I'd heard firsthand how much.

If Dennis and Mary Jo knew about a connection to a cartel, they'd probably both have side-by-side coronaries.

I'd pay good money to see that.

Sorry, Bobby. I guess even in an open and honest marriage, there are still some things best left unspoken.

Even with that knowledge, it didn't make me think any less of Amy. Actually, I respected her more for it. Her desire to conceal the relationship with her father was in order to protect it. A modern-day representation of the command to *honor thy father*.

Now me?

Okay, you can stop laughing.

Honoring my father would take more than... Ahem, more than....than...

Can I get back to you on that? After all the crap Frankie put me through over the years, this was gonna take more thought and put more strain on my gray matter than I had available right now.

Zeke's arm draped across my shoulders and ceased my musings. "Just thought you might want to know the man behind the woman Amy was."

I swiped my eyes. "Thanks, Zeke. I really appreciate you arranging this."

"So I guess you owe me now," he said with a nuzzle to my neck and a nibble to my ear.

"I don't think so," I corrected, trying not to let my legs give out from underneath me. "There's still the matter of two dollars and seventy cents you haven't reimbursed me for from getting Amy's records."

He sighed. "I don't carry change when I'm on duty. Too much jingling."

"Then I guess *you* still owe *me*."

Zeke gave me a devilish grin, kissed the top of my head then pulled me back into the crowded ballroom. "We always did make a good team."

Team?

Ho-boy.

That hit my intimacy radar quicker than a politician denying his latest scandal. Faster than a defensive end rushing the quarterback. Harder than the 'b' in *boyfriend*.

Do you think I'll ever get over my commitment issues? Don't answer that.

ABOUT THE AUTHOR

Sometimes life emulates fiction.

Life is filled with tragedy and Ms. Bale's writing reflects this reality. However, there is always a silver lining...even if one must spend their entire life searching for it.

In her previous career, Ms. Bale traveled the United States as a Government Relations Liaison, working closely with Congressional offices and various government agencies. This experience afforded her a glimpse into the sometimes "not so pretty" reality of the political sphere. Much of this reality and various locations throughout her travels make it into her writing.

She dreams of the day she can return to visit Alaska.

Connect with D. A. Bale online
Facebook: www.facebook/pages/D-A-Bale
Twitter: @DABale1
Blog: http://dabalepublishing.blogspot.com
Email: dabalepublishing@cox.net

www.ingramcontent.com/pod-product-compliance
Lightning Source LLC
Chambersburg PA
CBHW030152020625
27567CB00021BA/73